Please return on or before the latest date above.
You can renew online at *www.kent.gov.uk/libs*
or by telephone 08458 247 200

C155346077

CUSTOMER SERVICE EXCELLENCE

Libraries & Archives

00884\DTP\RN\07.07   LIB 7

THE CLUE OF THE GREEN CANDLE

Living in the village of Long Dene, best-selling novelist Roger Tempest is assisted by his secretary, Isabel Warren. When he unexpectedly disappears, private investigator Trevor Lowe is summoned. But eight days later, Tempest's body is found, dumped at a roadside. The police establish that it's murder and they suspect Richard, Tempest's impoverished brother and heir to his fortune. However, Lowe remains unconvinced — even when Richard escapes police custody and goes on the run. Then there is another murder . . .

GERALD VERNER

THE CLUE
OF THE
GREEN CANDLE

Complete and Unabridged

LINFORD
Leicester

First published in Great Britain

First Linford Edition
published 2012

British Library CIP Data

Verner, Gerald.
    The clue of the green candle. - -
(Linford mystery library)
1. Detective and mystery stories.
2. Large type books.
I. Title II. Series
823.9'12–dc23

ISBN 978–1–4448–1331–9

Published by
F. A. Thorpe (Publishing)
Anstey, Leicestershire

Set by Words & Graphics Ltd.
Anstey, Leicestershire
Printed and bound in Great Britain by
T. J. International Ltd., Padstow, Cornwall

This book is printed on acid-free paper

1

Roger Tempest Goes Out

'The door yielded under the pressure of Inspector Hayling's shoulder and he burst into the room. Samuel Inchpin lay sprawled on the floor, the hilt of a knife protruding from between his shoulder blades. He had been stabbed.'

Roger Tempest heaved a sigh of relief and reached for a cigarette.

'That'll be all, Miss Warren. We'll start the next chapter tomorrow morning,' he said.

His secretary raised a golden head from the notebook in which she had been furiously scribbling.

'Don't you think you ought to alter that last sentence, Mr. Tempest?' she asked.

'Alter it? Why?' demanded her employer, searching about on the littered desk in front of him for his matches.

'Well, it's a little obvious, don't you

1

think?' she said. 'I mean if there was a knife in his back he must have been stabbed.'

'Yes, I suppose you're right.' The novelist found his matches, struck one, and lit the cigarette that drooped from his lips. 'Yes, of course you're right. Change it to' — he wrinkled his brows, blew out a cloud of smoke, and stared at the ceiling — 'and it only needed one glance to see that he was dead.'

Isabel Warren made the alteration and closed her book. 'What about the instalment of that serial for *Fiction Weekly*,' she said, rising to her feet and brushing the creases from her neat tweed skirt. 'We promised they should have it by four o'clock tomorrow.'

Tempest made a wry grimace.

'Did we?' he muttered. 'Well, we'd better do it in the morning then. Damn these people! They always seem to be wanting an instalment. How much more of 'Red Fingers' have we got to do?'

She wrinkled her forehead and made a rapid calculation.

'Forty thousand words, roughly,' she answered.

'As much as that, eh?' he said frowning. 'We've got to deliver that on Saturday morning, and today's Wednesday. Oh, well, we'll do it somehow.'

'If you can do that instalment tonight — ' she began, but he shook his head.

'I'm not doing any more today!' he declared. 'We'll do that instalment in the morning and Stiller can run it up to Town.'

'Very well. I'll be in at nine,' she said. 'Good night, Mr. Tempest.'

'Good night, Miss Warren,' he replied, and as she left the cosily-furnished room, got up from the desk and strolled over to the fire.

Roger Tempest was a big man, with a smooth, reddish face and thin, greying, fair hair. During the hectic years which had followed the war — he had passed through the cataclysm unscathed — he had settled down to write for his living in earnest. Success had come to him suddenly and unexpectedly after many years of only moderate achievement. Beginning as a serious novelist he had, more for his amusement than because he expected any startling results, written a detective story. The reviewers had hailed it with a paean of praise, and, rather to his astonishment, he discovered that he was a 'best seller'. The flood of commissions forced him to engage a secretary, and after several more or less unsuccessful trials he discovered Isabel Warren.

She was the daughter of the local vicar, a bluff, hearty man, with whom Roger had struck up friendly relations almost immediately after his arrival in Long Dene, and it was pure accident that caused him to employ her in the first place. The girl who had been working for him was suddenly taken ill. Roger was in the midst of writing two serials and a series of short stories, all urgent commissions, and was at his wit's end. He confided his troubles to his friend the vicar, and that worthy man immediately suggested his daughter as a stopgap. Isabel had taken a course of shorthand and typewriting, and was used to dictation, for her father invariably dictated his sermons.

Roger had jumped at the opportunity,

and the girl had proved so successful that he had suggested she should remain permanently.

Successful, wealthy, a popular figure in the neighbourhood, Roger Tempest had only one worry to ripple the placid stream of his life, and that was his brother.

Richard was fifteen years his junior, and both in appearance and habits was in direct contrast to his brother. Whereas Roger was stoutish and fair, Richard was slim and dark. Unlike his brother, he detested books of every description, and loathed the country. His tastes were expensive, and, although on the death of their father they had each been left a similar income, Richard had realised the capital and run through his share in a year.

Again and again Roger had helped him out of some difficulty or other, but he quickly found that supplying his brother with money was rather like pouring water into a drain. It just slipped through his fingers. He was an inveterate gambler, and a well-known figure on the race-course. Roger had hoped once that as he grew older he might settle down to some profitable occupation, but as the years went by this hope faded.

He was thinking of his brother now as he stood smoking before the fire. Richard had telephoned that afternoon announcing his intention of dropping in during the evening, and Roger guessed that his reason was a financial one. This time, however, he told himself he would be firm. He would make Richard understand clearly, once and for all, that the goose had finished laying the golden eggs, and that in future he must curb his extravagance. It was not that he couldn't afford it, he was making big money and his own wants were simple, but it was bad for his brother's character.

There was a ring at the front door bell, and he heard the footsteps of Stiller, his servant, cross the hall to answer the summons. He guessed it was Richard before he heard his brother's cheery voice raised in greeting.

'Hello, Stiller! Beastly night! Raining like the devil. Is the feudal lord in?'

Stiller's reply was inaudible as Roger

went quickly over to the study door, and opened it.

'Come in, Dick!' he called. 'Stiller, bring drinks.'

'Ah, excellent suggestion,' remarked Dick Tempest, flinging his hat on the hall table and divesting himself of the belted motor coat he was wearing. 'Why in the world you live in these inaccessible regions beats me. Mud and wet and cold. Ugh! I've been skidding like the devil on these atrocious roads and — '

'It's a pity you had to choose today to come, Dick,' said Roger. 'I've got to go over to the Sheldons' to dinner. I tried to tell you that when you phoned, but you were in such a deuced hurry — '

'Couldn't help myself — coming today, I mean,' said his brother. 'I had to see you urgently.' He straightened up, helped himself to a cigarette from the box on the desk, and lit it. 'Fact of the matter is, old man I'm in rather a mess.'

'What, again?' said Roger.

Dick grinned without the least sign of embarrassment.

'I'm afraid so,' he answered. 'I've got to

find two thousand pounds by twelve o'clock tomorrow!'

'Well, I'm not going to do it!' declared Roger. 'I keep on supplying you with money which doesn't do any good at all.'

'Does all the good in the world, old boy!' said Dick. 'Now don't go and get stuffy! You always start off by saying you're not going to do this and you're not going to do that, and it's really a waste of time because you invariably do it in the end.'

'Well, I mean it this time!' said Roger stubbornly. 'You've really got to pull yourself together. It's not an earthly bit of good going on like this. I don't mind the money. It isn't that. But it's high time you realised that life isn't just a funfair.'

Dick sighed.

'I'm always realising it,' he remarked dolefully. 'There's nothing funny in losing two thousand on a dead cert.'

'I don't mean that, and you know I don't mean it!' said his brother impatiently. 'I wish you'd try and be serious!'

'I am serious,' said Dick. 'I've sent this feller off his cheque and there's only an overdraft of a hundred and seventy pounds to meet it.'

'Well, it'll have to go back!' said Roger. 'I'm not going to do any more until you decide to turn over a new leaf!'

A look of uneasiness came into the other's good-looking face. 'I say! You don't mean that, Roger?' he said anxiously.

'I do!' declared Roger firmly. 'I mean every word of it!'

'But, my dear old chap,' protested Dick, 'it's going to put me in a deuced awkward position!'

'I'm not grudging you anything,' said Roger. 'I'm quite willing to finance you in any occupation you like to choose. But I do want you to do something instead of just frittering away your life in this stupid manner. However, this time I'm firm. I'm not letting you have a penny until you've decided to alter your views!'

His tone was so emphatic that his brother was alarmed.

'Oh, come Roger!' he said. 'You don't mean that? I'm going to be in a frightful mess if this cheque isn't met. It's a debt of honour!'

'Well, you should have thought of that before you incurred it!' said Roger determinedly. 'The whole trouble, Dick, is that it's been too easy. You just go drifting on, get yourself in a hole, and come to me to get you out, and I've always done it. I'm not going to do it any more.'

His brother swallowed his drink at a gulp and looked at him steadily.

'I really believe you mean that,' he said quietly, and his face had gone a little pale.

'I do mean it!' retorted Roger. 'And now I'll have to go and dress, unless I want to be late at the Sheldons'.' He glanced at the clock.

'I'll drop you there if you like,' said Dick in a subdued voice. 'You won't change your mind — just this once?'

'No, I won't!' said Roger, and then, he paused at the door: 'Unless you agree to try and become a useful member of society.'

He hurried upstairs to his bedroom, and all the while he was shaving and dressing he steeled himself to stick to his decision.

He came down to find his brother

talking to Stiller in the hall.

'You needn't wait up for me,' he said to the servant. 'I shall probably be late. Leave the whiskey and soda.'

'Very good, sir,' said Stiller, and helped him on with his coat, the last service, although he didn't know it, he was ever to render his master.

'Ready?' said Dick, and they passed out into the wet darkness of the night — for Roger Tempest the last time he was to cross that hospitable threshold!

2

Trevor Lowe Receives a Visitor

'The gentleman,' said the maid, 'is waiting.'

Trevor Lowe took the card from the salver and glanced at it. In neat copper plate he saw the inscription 'Bruce Hammerton, 128b, Arundel Street, Strand, W.C.1.'

'Bruce Hammerton,' he murmured, thoughtfully. 'The name seems familiar, and yet I can't place it.'

'He's a fat little gentleman with a bald head, sir,' said the maid helpfully, 'and glasses on his nose.'

'I am afraid that still conveys nothing to me,' murmured the dramatist. 'Ask him to come in.'

He laid the card down on the desk as the servant departed, and frowned slightly, trying to cudgel his memory in an effort to recollect in what circumstances he had heard the name of the caller before. He was still unsuccessful when Mr. Hammerton was shown in.

The maid's unflattering description had been fairly accurate. Mr. Hammerton was stout and round; the shining dome of his head was devoid of hair, and on the bridge of his small, thick nose, he wore a pair of rimless glasses.

'Good morning, sir,' he greeted. 'I must apologise for calling without making an appointment, but the matter is of some urgency, and therefore I decided to risk it.'

'Sit down, Mr. Hammerton,' said the dramatist, pushing forward a chair. 'I seem to remember your name, but I can't at the moment recall where we met.'

'I think we met casually some time ago,' said the visitor as he sat down carefully, and hitched up his immaculately creased trousers, 'at one of Coyles literary lunches. If you remember you were the guest of honour — '

Lowe's face cleared.

'That's it!' he said. 'You're Mr. Bruce Hammerton, the literary agent. I remember now! What can I do for you, Mr. Hammerton?'

'Well,' said the stout man, hesitantly, 'the matter is of some delicacy. The fact of the matter is Mr. Roger Tempest has disappeared.'

Lowe raised his eyebrows. There was no need for him to ask who Roger Tempest was. It would have been equal to inquiring the identity of the Prime Minister.

'Suppose you tell me more about it,' said Lowe, crossing to his desk and seating himself. 'When did Mr. Tempest disappear?'

'Eight days ago,' answered the literary agent. 'He left his house at half past seven on a Wednesday evening to keep a dinner engagement with some people called Sheldon who live in the same village. He was driven to the Sheldons' by his brother and spent the evening there, leaving shortly after twelve. That is the last that has been seen of him. He left the Sheldons' but he never returned home. When his secretary arrived at nine o'clock the following morning in order to work on the instalment of the serial I mentioned, she was informed by Mr. Tempest's servant, a man called Stiller, who has been in his employ some considerable time that his master was not in the house and had not come home the previous night. Since then, although we have instituted careful inquiries among all his friends, nothing has been seen or heard of him.'

'Was there anything, to your knowledge, any trouble or unpleasantness in his past history that might offer a reason for this sudden disappearance?' asked the dramatist.

The literary agent shook his head.

'Nothing at all!' he declared. 'He was a very quiet studious man, of simple tastes. His only hobby was golf and his work. He has a very charming house at Long Dene, in Berkshire, and he only came up to town when it was absolutely essential from a business point of view.'

'Was he married?' said Lowe.

'No. He was a bachelor,' answered Mr. Hammerton.

'Had there been any tragedy in his life, a love affair that had gone astray?'

Again the literary agent replied in the negative.

'He hadn't been overworking recently?' asked Lowe.

'Not more than usual,' said Mr. Hammerton. 'His output was of course prodigious, but it never seemed to affect him adversely. He had a tremendous capacity for sustained work.'

'And so far as you're aware he had no worries, financial or otherwise?' queried Lowe.

'Certainly not financial!' answered the literary agent. 'At his request I superintend all his financial affairs, and there is a balance at his bank of nearly ten thousand pounds. I am almost equally sure that he had no personal worries.'

'These people you mentioned, whom he dined with, on the night of his disappearance,' said the dramatist, 'are they aware that he is missing?'

'Oh, yes,' said the literary agent. 'They had to be informed. So, of course, do Miss Warren, his secretary, and his servant, Stiller, know, and they are exceedingly worried. They agreed with me that secrecy, at the present juncture, was most necessary. That was what made me come to you instead of going to the police.'

'I think I had better see them,' said Lowe, and jotted down the names and addresses which Mr. Hammerton gave him. 'You also mentioned something about a brother. I should like to see him too.'

'Mr. Richard Tempest,' said Mr. Hammerton. 'He has a flat in Half Moon Street. A rather harum-scarum gentleman, from what I can gather.'

His tone was disapproving. Obviously, thought Lowe, Richard Tempest was not a favourite with the literary agent.

'And it was he who drove the missing man to the Sheldons'?' he said,

Mr. Hammerton nodded.

'Yes. He had gone down to see his brother,' he answered, 'with a view, I presume, although I have no exact knowledge, of extracting money from him.'

'Was he dependent on his brother then?' said the dramatist.

'Almost entirely!' declared the literary agent. 'In fact, Tempest was a great deal too generous. He would have been far better advised in my opinion, if he'd made his brother earn his living instead of encroaching on his generosity.'

'You have, of course, seen the brother?'

'Oh, yes,' said Mr. Hammerton. 'But he is as much mystified as any of us. He can suggest no reason for the disappearance.'

'Well, I'll do what I can,' said Lowe. 'And if I discover anything I'll let you know immediately.'

The literary agent rose to his feet and held out his hand.

'Thank you very much,' he said. 'I am infinitely obliged to you.'

'Goodbye,' said Lowe, 'I hope you will have cause to be.'

When the worried man had taken his departure, he sat down at his desk and read through the notes he had made. They were meagre in the extreme. It would be necessary to see the brother, Richard Tempest, and also the people at Long Dene who had been the last to see Roger Tempest before his disappearance. Not that he expected to learn much from either. Mr. Hammerton had already exhausted any information that might be forthcoming in those quarters.

3

Roger Tempest Comes Back

Leaving a message for Arnold White to say where he had gone, the dramatist took a taxi and drove to Half Moon Street.

His interview with Richard Tempest resulted, as he had expected, in supplying him with very little further information than he possessed already. The novelist's brother was worried and anxious, but he confirmed Mr. Hammerton's assertion that Roger Tempest had had no personal reason that might have led to his voluntary disappearance.

Returning to Portland Place he lunched, explained to his interested secretary the gist of the new business on which he was engaged, and taking his car drove down in the afternoon to Long Dene.

The White House, Tempest's bungalow-cottage, lay on the outskirts of the village, and he was received by Isabel Warren. The girl looked worried and harassed, as well she might, for she had spent the last eight days in trying desperately to cope with the numerous messages and telephone calls, which were arriving hourly. Frantic editors were clamouring for overdue copy, interviewers were demanding to know when Mr. Tempest could be seen; a film company who had commissioned a scenario were growing steadily angrier and angrier.

'It's dreadful, Mr. Lowe,' said the girl helplessly. 'I don't know what to say to these people. I've told them Mr. Tempest is away for a few days, but unless he returns I don't know what will happen. Already they have had to find somebody else to continue his serial for *Fiction Weekly*.'

'He never hinted that he was likely to be going away?' said the dramatist.

She shook her head.

'I don't think he had any idea of it,' she said. 'He couldn't have done, we were far too busy! I'm certain that Mr. Tempest is not staying away of his own accord! I'm convinced that something very serious has happened to him.'

'How far away is the Sheldons' house?' asked Lowe.

'About a mile and a half,' she answered. 'We're on one side of the village, and their house is on the other. The vicarage, where I live, is midway between.'

'I presume,' continued Lowe, 'that since Mr. Tempest's brother drove him over he would have walked back?'

'He did,' she answered. 'Or rather he set out to walk back. Mr. Sheldon told us that.'

'What time did he leave?' asked the dramatist.

'Ten minutes past twelve,' said the girl.

'Is it a straight road?' he inquired.

'Practically straight,' she answered.

'So that he ought to have arrived here at about twenty-to-one at the latest?' he went on, frowning.

She nodded.

'I suppose,' said Lowe, 'you haven't inquired whether anybody saw him?'

'Very few people in Long Dene are awake at that hour,' she said, with a smile. 'But, so far as I've been able to ascertain, nobody saw him.'

'And the fact that he hadn't come home wasn't discovered until the morning?' he said.

She shook her head.

There was a short silence during which the dramatist stroked his chin thoughtfully.

'These people, the Sheldons,' he said presently. 'Are they old friends of Mr. Tempest's?'

'No. I should hardly call them that,' she answered. 'They've only been here about eighteen months. Mr. Sheldon's a very nice man, and his wife's charming. Mr. Tempest's disappearance has worried them terribly.'

'It's an extraordinary thing altogether,' remarked Lowe. 'It seems impossible, in the circumstances, to suppose that he's absenting himself of his own free will. Perhaps I could have a word with Stiller?'

The servant was sent for, and Lowe put a number of questions. But the man's answers did nothing to augment his knowledge. He was obviously distressed, and just as puzzled as the rest of them.

'You can take it from me, sir,' he said emphatically at the end of the interview, 'that something happened to him! Mr. Tempest would never have gone without a word unless he couldn't have helped himself.'

There was nothing further to be learned at the White House, and Lowe set off to see the Sheldons.

The house in which they lived was an imposing mansion standing in its own grounds, and approached by a winding drive that ran between an avenue of beech trees.

Mr. Sheldon was a stout, jovial-faced little man, who gave Lowe the impression of being a retired tradesman, which he discovered later was very far removed from the truth. Mr. Sheldon was neither retired nor a tradesman. He was, in fact, an architect. He had offices off the Strand, and conducted a flourishing business designing blocks of flats and similar properties.

'It's completely beyond me!' he said, when he had ensconced the dramatist in a comfortable chair in a cosy room that was half smoking room, half library. 'Completely beyond me! Tempest was in the best of spirits when he left here. I offered to send him home in the car, but he jokingly remarked that his waistline was getting a little too prominent, and the exercise would do him good. What could have happened to him goodness only knows!' He pinched a fold of skin below his chin and shook his head.

'He didn't say anything, in the course of the evening, that might have suggested he was going away?'

'Nothing at all!' declared Mr. Sheldon. 'In fact quite the contrary. He asked my wife and me over to dinner on the following Saturday. When I was told he hadn't returned home I was amazed. Completely amazed!'

He obviously knew nothing that was likely to be of value to the investigation into Roger Tempest's disappearance, and after accepting a drink and being introduced to Mrs. Sheldon, a dark-haired, pretty woman, several years younger than her husband, Lowe took his departure.

He drove back to the White House

slowly, following the road that the missing man must have taken on that night when he had walked into oblivion. It was, as Isabel Warren had said, perfectly safe, and without any danger points whereby a man, walking in the dark, could have come to harm. A thick wood bordered it on one side, and on the other a high hedge separated the road itself from the meadows and ploughed fields. Before reaching the village it dipped into a hollow, rising on the other side to join Long Dene High Street.

At the bottom of the decline, his headlights picked out a little knot of people standing close to the grassy edge on the woodland side. He saw the glint of a bicycle, and the unmistakable helmet of a policeman, and slowed as he drew level. They were bending over something, and the policeman straightened up and turned as he stopped the car.

'Now then,' he said in an authoritative voice, 'move on there!'

'What is it?' asked the dramatist. 'An accident?'

'No, it's murder!' replied a labourer.

25

'Mr. Tempest, the owner of the White House — '

'That'll do, Raikes!' said the constable sharply. 'Move your car on, sir, please!'

But Lowe was already stepping from the driving seat on to the roadway.

'Did I understand you to say that Mr. Tempest had been found murdered?' he asked sharply.

'I didn't say anything,' said the constable. 'I'll trouble you, sir, if you don't mind, not to interfere!'

'I am a friend of Mr. Tempest's,' said the dramatist, not strictly truthfully. 'What has happened, officer?'

The constable was clearly rather doubtful how to handle the situation.

'If you're a friend of Mr. Tempest's, sir,' he said reluctantly, 'I suppose that makes a difference. P'raps you'd better wait until the Inspector comes. I've sent along to notify him, and he should be here any minute.'

'I should like to see your Inspector,' said the dramatist. 'How did you find Mr. Tempest? And what makes you think he's been murdered?'

'I found 'im,' put in the labourer who had spoken before. 'There ain't no doubt about 'is bein' murdered, Mister. Look at 'im!'

The constable began a protest, but Lowe stepped to the man's side and looked down at the thing that lay on the ragged grass edging the road. It was the sprawling body of a middle-aged man; a stubbly growth of beard covered face and chin, and the evening clothes were stained and creased. The crumpled shirtfront was stained, too, but more ominously, a reddish brown stain that had spread in an ugly patch round the narrow slit in the left breast!

4

Inspector Mirren Takes Charge

'Give me a little more light, will you?'

The middle-aged man in the soiled mackintosh who was kneeling in the roadway spoke sharply without turning his head.

'Move aside there, Paley! And you, too, Raikes! That better, Doctor?'

Inspector Mirren looked towards the stooping man, saw him nod, and turned to Trevor Lowe.

'Mysterious business, sir,' he said. 'I can't understand anyone wanting to harm Mr. Tempest.'

'I suppose there's no doubt it is Mr. Tempest?' said the dramatist.

'No doubt at all!' declared the Inspector. 'Even with that beard I'd recognise him immediately. Poor chap! He used to come and chat to me at the station for hours on end. Interested in crime he was.

Wrote some good books, too. I've read most of 'em.' He shook his head sadly. 'Oh, well! He won't write any more, poor feller!'

He had arrived, accompanied by the doctor and a sergeant, a few minutes after Lowe had discovered the little group by the body. The dramatist had explained who he was, and Mirren, a burly, genial-faced man, had welcomed his presence. The police car had been turned so that the headlights illumined the scene, bathing the doctor and the grim object over which he bent in a white glare that threw distorted shadows onto the gaunt trunks of the leafless trees that clustered in the vicinity.

The doctor finished his examination and rose to his feet, brushing the mud from his trousers.

'Well, he's dead, of course. Been dead for nearly twelve hours, as far as I can say. He was stabbed with a thin-bladed knife that seems to have pierced the heart. That would account for all this blood.'

'Twelve hours, eh?' murmured Lowe, and the doctor nodded.

'Within an hour either way,' he amended. 'I wouldn't go nearer than that.'

'Queer!' said Mirren, frowning. 'He couldn't have been lying here all that time — '

'He wasn't!' interrupted the dramatist. 'He wasn't here an hour ago. I passed this way myself, and if he'd been here then I should have seen him.'

'There's another remarkable fact,' put in the doctor. 'I daresay you've noticed. He's in evening clothes. He was wearing them when he was killed. It's now eight o'clock, which means if he was killed twelve hours ago he was wearing evening dress in the morning.'

'I think I can explain that,' said Lowe, quietly.

He drew the Inspector away out of earshot of the curious villagers and briefly explained the situation. Mirren pursed his lips in a silent whistle.

'Been missing for eight days, has he?' he said. 'Well, that's a funny thing. I thought I hadn't seen 'im about. But where could he have been until now?'

30

'That's one of the things we've got to find out,' said the dramatist. 'And somehow I don't think it's going to be an easy task. Wherever Tempest was between the time he left the Sheldons' house, and now, it was where he was killed. He was brought to this place and his body left here. The doctor's evidence of the time of death clearly shows that he wasn't killed here!'

'Yes, that seems clear enough, sir.' Inspector Mirren scratched his chin. 'It's about the only thing that is clear,' he added. 'Why weren't the police informed when it was found he was missing?'

'Because nobody was certain,' explained Lowe, 'that he hadn't gone away of his own accord. You quite realise that if he'd had some private reason for absenting himself a police inquiry might have proved very embarrassing. Naturally, neither his literary agent nor his secretary nor his brother would wish to take the responsibility for such an action.'

'No, I see that,' said Mirren. 'Still, it's a pity, all the same. We might have been able to prevent this.' He looked over towards the sprawling figure, and shook his head. 'Just like a bit out of one of his own books,' he muttered.

'You won't want me any more?' The doctor's voice broke the short silence that followed. 'I've got a waiting room full of patients, and — '

'That's all right, Doctor,' said Mirren. 'Let me have a report in the morning, will you?'

The doctor nodded and moved rapidly away.

'Well, we'd better have a look through his clothing,' said the Inspector. 'Maybe we'll find something that 'ull give us a clue to where he's been.'

But his hope was not justified. There was nothing at all in the dead man's pockets. Everything portable had been removed, including his wallet and watch. Lowe made a discovery, however, and pointed it out to the Inspector.

'Look at his wrists,' he murmured, and Mirren peered interestedly at the red marks.

'Looks as though he'd been tied up,' he said. 'The skin's all chafed and raw.'

Lowe nodded.

'That's the conclusion I came to,' he said. He transferred his attention to the dead man's ankles, undoing his suspenders and turning down the thin, black socks. 'Yes,' he announced. 'There are similar marks here. It leaves very little doubt, in my opinion, that during the time he was absent he was kept prisoner somewhere.'

'But why?' demanded the Inspector. 'What for? Why should anybody want to kidnap Mr. Tempest? I could understand it if there'd been a demand for ransom, or something like that, but there hasn't been anything of the sort, has there?'

'Oh, no, it's not as simple as that,' said the dramatist. 'There's something much more behind it.'

Inspector Mirren was clearly bewildered.

'Well, it beats me!' he declared. 'If somebody wanted to kill him why didn't they kill him at once? Why keep him tied up all that time?'

'The suggestion seems to be,' remarked Lowe, 'that they kept him till they'd got something they wanted. And then, when he was no longer useful to them, they killed him.'

'And dumped his body by the side of this road,' muttered Mirren. 'They must have brought it in a car.'

'Yes, I think you can take that as a certainty,' said Lowe.

The Inspector sighed.

'Well, sir,' he said, 'it's early days yet to talk, but it looks to me as if this was going to be a mighty teaser.'

'I agree with you,' answered the dramatist. 'There doesn't seem to be the slightest trace of a clue to the identity of the murderer.'

'Or to the motive,' said Mirren. 'That's what we've got to look for first. Mr. Tempest was fairly well off, and I remember 'is tellin' me once that he hadn't any living relations except this brother you mentioned. I s'pose he'll come in for whatever there is?'

Lowe looked at him sharply. So that was the line the Inspector's thoughts were taking? Well, it was the obvious one, of course. If Roger Tempest had died without leaving a will —

'From all accounts the brother is a bit flighty,' went on Mirren. 'Gamblin' and suchlike.' He shrugged his shoulders. 'Oh, well, this is not the place or the time to discuss that,' he said abruptly. 'I'll have to see about getting the body to the mortuary. Are you staying in the district, sir?'

Lowe shook his head.

'No,' he replied. 'I only came to look into the matter of Tempest's disappearance at the request of his literary agent. There's nothing further I can do, so I shall be going back to London tonight.'

Mirren looked a little disappointed.

'Oh, will you, sir?' he said. 'Well, of course, as you say, there's nothing to keep you. It won't even be necessary for you to attend the inquest.' He hesitated. 'I wonder if you'd mind notifyin' Miss Warren of what's 'appened,' he added apologetically. 'That's if it won't be putting you out.'

'Certainly I will,' said Lowe quickly, 'and it won't be putting me out at all. I shouldn't have left without saying good-bye to Miss Warren in any case.'

'Thank you very much, sir,' said the Inspector gratefully. 'It will help me a lot.'

The dramatist shook hands with him and went over to his car. As he drove off he saw the constable ride furiously away on his bicycle and guessed that he had gone for the ambulance. The news of the discovery had already spread, for he passed a straggling line of people hastening from the direction of the village, chattering and whispering excitedly as they hurried along. The crime would cause a sensation, not only in the district where he had lived, but throughout the world, for Roger Tempest had been a celebrity. The newspapers would seize on the mysterious circumstances surrounding his death, and his publishers would reap the reward of an unexpected boom of publicity.

He drew up at the White House and, when Stiller opened the door before he could ring, he saw by the servant's face that there was no necessity to break the news. The man already knew.

'Miss Warren's father telephoned, sir,' said Stiller, and his voice was husky with emotion. 'She has gone over to the vicarage. I — I can't believe it, sir. It's dreadful! Who could have done it? Who could have wanted to harm Mr. Tempest? He never said or did an unkind thing to anyone.'

Lowe drove back to London with that epitaph running through his mind. 'He never said or did an unkind thing to anyone.' Surely no better could be said of any man? And yet Roger Tempest had died violently and horribly — murdered by an unknown hand for an unknown reason.

5

The Inquest

Trevor Lowe had been right when he had concluded that the murder of Roger Tempest would provide a first class sensation. It did. The day following the discovery of the body every newspaper carried a front-page story, with a photograph of the section of the road, and another of the murdered man. Inside was a hastily written biography, with more photographs. The day after, every bookstall and bookshop was loaded with the novels that had made Tempest famous. The libraries filled their windows with displays of his books, and the publishers had to engage a special staff to deal with the orders that poured in from every part of the country.

With all this tremendous publicity it was not surprising that the small school-room in which the inquest was held should have been packed out long before the inquiry was due to begin. Many people had come long distances by car, and, since it was only possible to accommodate a limited number, the majority were disappointed. The Press was well represented, and Lowe saw many familiar faces when he at last succeeded, with the assistance of Inspector Mirren, in forcing his way through the crowd and gaining admission to the improvised courtroom.

'I didn't expect to see you here today, sir,' whispered the Inspector, as he found the dramatist a seat near the Coroner's table.

'I'm afraid I couldn't resist the temptation,' said Lowe with a smile. 'I suppose I'm lucky to have got in at all?'

'You are, sir,' said Mirren, glancing round the crowded room. 'Why didn't you let me know you were coming?'

'Because I didn't know myself until the last minute,' was the reply. 'I suppose this will be a very short affair? Just the usual evidence of identification and the cause of death, and then you'll ask for an adjournment, eh?'

Inspector Mirren looked at him strangely.

'I think there'll be a bit more than that, sir,' he said slowly, and Lowe raised his eyebrows.

'That means there have been developments,' he murmured. 'What have you got up your sleeve, Inspector?'

Before Mirren could reply the Coroner came bustling in and took his place at the table. He was a thin man with a bald head, and a fringe of greying hair, with a long, high-bridged nose, very red at the tip, and narrow eyes that were almost completely hidden under bushy brows. He was afflicted with a hard, dry cough, and a nervous habit of passing his fingers quickly over his long upper lip every few minutes.

The jury had by now all been sworn in, and when they had retired and viewed the body, the Coroner began his introductory speech.

It was short and to the point. He outlined, briefly, the reason for the inquiry, touched lightly on the worldwide reputation of the deceased, and, without further preliminary, proceeded to call the first witness, Richard Tempest.

Rather white and ill-at-ease, Richard took the stand.

'You have seen the body of the deceased,' said the Coroner, when he had been sworn and his name and address been recorded. 'Do you identify it as that of your elder brother, Roger Tempest?'

'Yes.'

'You were in the habit of seeing your brother frequently?'

'Yes.'

'When was the last time you saw him alive?'

'Eleven days ago — on the evening of Wednesday, March the 12th.'

'Where did you see him?'

'At his house — The White House. I called there in the early evening.'

'What time did you leave him?'

'I don't remember the exact time. He was going out to dinner with some friends. I drove him to the house and left him.'

'And that was the last time you saw your brother alive?'

'Yes.'

'What did you do after you had left him

at his friends' house?'

'I went back to London.'

'Immediately?'

'Yes.'

'During the time you were with your brother did you notice any difference in him?'

'I don't understand what you mean.'

'Was he in his usual spirits?'

'Oh, I see. Yes, I didn't notice any difference.'

'What kind of terms were you on with your brother?'

'What kind of terms?'

'That's what I said, Mr. Tempest.'

'The best. We were the best of friends.'

The Coroner consulted his notes, made a careful entry, and looked up.

'That is all I wish to ask you at present, Mr. Tempest,' he said. 'I shall most likely want to recall you later, so please don't leave the courtroom.'

Richard returned to his place, and the Coroner called Doctor Thornton.

The new witness was the doctor whom Mirren had brought with him after being notified of the discovery of Roger

Tempest's body by the constable. He was a small, dapper man, very brisk and business-like. He deposed that his name was Walter Thornton, that he was a qualified medical practitioner, and police surgeon for the district.

His evidence was given in a curt, professional manner, and was very brief. He merely repeated what Lowe had already heard him tell Inspector Mirren. Miss Warren was next called and then Stiller was sworn.

His evidence was more or less a repetition of the girl's, and he was quickly dismissed. So far, thought Lowe, nothing of a sensational nature had come to light. Whatever Inspector Mirren had up his sleeve was being reserved for later in the inquiry.

The next witness was the genial-faced Mr. Sheldon. He deposed that Roger Tempest had left his house at a few minutes after eleven o'clock, and had insisted on walking to his own home. He had appeared to be quite himself during the evening, and had exhibited no signs of mental distress. He had mentioned nothing at all about going away, in fact, on the contrary, he had stated that he was exceedingly busy at that period, and had declined a suggestion on the witness's part that they should meet for a round of golf on the following Saturday morning. He had vouchsafed, in explanation for this refusal, that he intended to work over the weekend in order to clear up some arrears, remarking that he was very much behind with two of his contracts. This was the only contribution Mr. Sheldon could offer. Having given his evidence clearly and concisely, and been thanked by the Coroner, he left the stand, and his place was taken by Mr. Hammerton.

The literary agent looked a little worried and nervous, but he answered the questions put to him without hesitation. After explaining his exact position in relation to the dead man, he went on, at the Coroner's request, to give a detailed statement of Roger Tempest's literary affairs. The Coroner's bushy brows rose when he learned of the large sums that were involved.

'The deceased at the time of his death

must have been a very rich man?' he remarked.

'He was certainly quite well off,' answered the literary agent cautiously. 'He must have been worth something in the region of one hundred and twenty thousand pounds. His income from America was nearly fifteen thousand a year, the royalties on his English contracts was a sum more than double that, and there were a great number of foreign rights as well that brought in quite respectable sums.'

The Coroner was obviously impressed.

'I had no idea that such an enormous sum was involved,' he said. 'I presume that a great portion of this income will continue?'

'I estimate that it will be even larger,' replied Mr. Hammerton. 'The tremendous public interest which this terrible affair has aroused is sure to have the effect of increased sales, and I don't think I should be far out if I said that they would be almost double.'

'Was the deceased an extravagant man?'

'No, quite the reverse. He had very little time to be extravagant, and his tastes were of the simplest. I don't suppose he spent more than four or at the outside five thousand a year.'

'Then the greater part of his earnings has accumulated?'

'Yes.'

'Thank you, Mr. Hammerton. That is all I wish to ask you at present.'

The literary agent retired, and the Coroner consulted his notes. Lowe pursed his lips. He was beginning to see where all these questions were leading.

The next witness was the dead man's lawyer, Mr. Whittlesey. He was a stoutish, rather imposing person, and he took the stand with an assurance acquired by long practice.

'For how long have you acted as legal adviser to the deceased?' asked the Coroner, when the usual formalities had been attended to.

'For just over ten years.'

'Then you must know a great deal about his private affairs?'

'I do.'

'Can you suggest any reason for the violent nature of his death?'

'No.'

'Did the deceased attend to his own financial business or did you look after it for him?'

'I looked after his investments. Mr. Hammerton, his agent, was responsible for his literary contracts.'

'Quite so. You will be able to tell us, then, the approximate value of the estate?'

'Yes. It is very much larger than Mr. Hammerton estimated. The total amount is, roughly, a quarter of a million.'

'Dear me, that is really a colossal sum.' The Coroner shook his head as though he found it difficult to believe there was so much money in the world. Did the deceased leave a will?'

'Yes.'

'Has probate been applied for?'

'Yes.'

'Then there can be no objection to disclosing the terms of the will?'

'None. The principal beneficiaries are: Miss Warren, who benefits to the extent of five thousand pounds, James Stiller, who receives one thousand pounds, and Mr. Richard Tempest, the deceased's brother, who receives one hundred thousand pounds, and is also the residuary legatee.'

The quietly spoken words caused a mild sensation. A low whisper ran through the crowded room, and Lowe saw the jury glance significantly at one another. Here was a definite and tangible motive. By his brother's death Richard Tempest had become a rich man. And he had been in the district on the very evening that Roger had disappeared, and there was only his word to prove that he had gone back to London when he had said. The dramatist's eyes narrowed. Was this going to turn out a very simple case after all? Evidently Inspector Mirren thought so. It was easy to see what he was working for — a verdict of wilful murder against Richard. But, if he hoped to get it, he must be in possession of further and more conclusive evidence than he had yet disclosed. At present there was nothing to warrant more than a vague suspicion, scarcely even that.

The Coroner put several more questions to Mr. Whittlesey, concerning the will, and then called Inspector Mirren.

Trevor Lowe leaned forward attentively as the inspector stepped alertly to the stand. In a few minutes he would learn what it was that Mirren had held up his sleeve.

6

The Verdict

The Inspector took the oath, and as he waited for the Coroner's first question Lowe caught a brief glance, flicked in his direction, that said clearly: 'Now you're going to hear something!'

The opening stages of the examination, however, were uneventful enough. The usual questions were put concerning Mirren's name, rank and the circumstances in which he had come into the case. After this the Coroner consulted his notes, coughed, passed the first two fingers of his right hand rapidly and nervously across his upper lip, and raised his eyes.

'Now Inspector.' he said, 'it has been suggested that Mr. Tempest was murdered elsewhere, and that his body was brought afterwards to the place where it was found. Do you agree with that?'

'Yes, sir,' answered Mirren; 'I don't think there can be any doubt about it.'

'Will you give the court your reasons for thinking so?'

'I ascertained that several people who had passed along the road a few hours before had seen no sign of the body. From the medical evidence the knife-wound which killed the deceased was inflicted some considerable time before the earliest at which the body could have been deposited at the spot where it was found.'

The Coroner glanced at the jury and then down at the papers in front of him.

'The deceased had been missing for eight days,' he said, after a pause. 'During your investigations have you discovered any evidence that suggests where he may have been?'

'No, sir, but I found evidence which leads me to believe that the deceased was detained somewhere against his will.'

'What is this evidence to which you refer?'

'The deceased had a growth of beard which indicated that he had not shaved for several days, his clothes were in such a condition as to suggest that he had not taken them off for a long time, his face and hands were very dirty. Apart from this there were marks on his wrists and ankles that appear to have been caused by their being tightly bound.'

'H'm!' The Coroner cleared his throat. 'It would appear, then, that the body was brought to the place where it was found in some vehicle. Were there any indications to suggest this, or to suggest the kind of vehicle used?'

'No, sir.'

The Coroner brushed his fingers quickly over his mouth, as though he were removing an invisible fly, and consulted a slip of paper.

'I understand, however,' he said, looking up over the tops of his glasses, 'that you have important fresh evidence to put before this Court?'

'Yes, sir,' answered the Inspector, and produced a black notebook the pages of which he turned rapidly. There was a stir of renewed interest throughout the room. Now it's coming, thought Lowe, Mirren is about to spring his bombshell.

'I have discovered a very important new witness, sir,' went on the Inspector, 'a man who actually saw the deceased after he had left Mr. Sheldon's house.'

'Where did this witness you mention see the deceased?' inquired the Coroner.

'He was standing a few yards from the spot where his body was found,' replied Mirren, 'and he was talking to another man who was seated in a car!'

A sigh ran through the little courtroom like a breath of wind. Excited whispers rose above the rustle of papers from the Press benches. The sensation, which everybody present had been hoping for, had come at last. Who was this new witness — and, more important — who was the man to whom Roger Tempest had been speaking on that lonely road on the night of his disappearance?

The Coroner looked angrily around, and the whispers were stilled.

'This is very interesting, and of the utmost importance, Inspector,' he said. 'You can produce this witness now?'

'Yes, sir, he's with one of my men outside.'

'Who is he?

'A man named George Saunders, sir, a local resident, and a farmhand on Mr. Arbuthnot's farm.'

'Ah, yes, yes,' the Coroner nodded several times very quickly. 'I know Mr. Arbuthnot well.' He turned to an official at his side. 'Have this man Saunders brought in at once.'

The clerk departed, pushing his way through the crowd, and the Coroner once more turned his attention to Mirren.

'I think I will postpone putting any further questions to you, Inspector,' he said, 'until after I have heard the evidence of this new witness.'

Mirren bowed and left the stand, shooting a glance at Lowe as he went back to his place.

A door at the back of the room opened, and a constable forced his way in urging forward a shambling figure in a greasy black jacket and stained corduroy trousers tucked into battered leather gaiters. The round, red face of this individual was as battered as the gaiters, and looked as though it had braved every kind of weather, as indeed it had. A stubble of grey whisker, which seemed to emphasise the twinkle in the faded blue eyes, circled the face and was lost in the thick mop of tousled white hair. As he saw every eye turned towards him, this old man, who had lived in Long Dene ever since he could remember, squared his broad shoulders, and stumped down the gangway that was made for him, beaming at all and sundry, obviously more concerned with the fact that this was his hour than with the gravity of the occasion.

He took the oath with great solemnity, and the Coroner cleared his throat.

'Your name is George Saunders, and you live at Ivy Cottage, Long Dene?' he said.

'Aye, sir, you know that very well without needin' ter ask,' replied the old man. 'Everybody knows Garge Saunders in these parts. Oi've lived 'ere, man an' boy, all me loife an' — '

'Yes, yes, Saunders. Please confine yourself to just answering the questions put to you. We are inquiring into the death of Mr. Roger Tempest, whom I believe you knew?'

'Aye, I did that, an' a real nice gentleman 'e was too — '

'I understand,' broke in the Coroner, 'that you saw Mr. Tempest on the night he is believed to have disappeared, talking to someone on the Minchester Road?'

'Aye, that be right,' agreed old George.

'Will you tell us as briefly as possible the circumstances in which you saw the deceased?'

'Eh?' The old man looked a little bewildered, and the Coroner repeated his question more sharply.

'Well, sir, it were like this,' he began, scratching his head and frowning deeply. 'Oi'd bin o'er ter Barton that night. It were the final o' the Barton darts champeenship, an' oi were ter meet ol' Tom 'Itchens for t' final. A grand game it was, too, an' oi beat ol' Tom good an' proper!' He uttered a reminiscent chuckle. 'Aye, good an' proper! Even if oi am nigh on seventy oi can still throw a tidy dart!' He beamed at the assembly, and the Coroner gently reminded him to get on with his story. 'Well, sur, seein' as I was the champeen,' went on old George, determined to drive this point thoroughly home, 'it were decided to have a sort of celeb'ation. We all 'ad a pint or two, an' it were getting late when oi started for to walk back to Long Dene. Oi bain't as young as I were, an oi don't walk so fast, an' it must have been 'alf-past 'leven when oi were coming along the Minchester road. Oi were about a mile from 'ome when oi sees a moty car pulled up 'longside t'road. As oi came closer oi sees there's two fellows with it, one sitting in the car and t'other standin' beside it. Oi didn't reckernise 'em then, but oi 'eard 'em for they was quarrellin'. Raisin' their voices so as you could 'ear 'em a good way away, though you couldn't tell what was bein' said. When oi comes up with 'em they stops, an' then oi sees that the one standin' in t'road be Mr. Tempest. Oi gives 'im a 'Good night' as oi goes by, an' 'e replies pleasant-like. An' oi goes on. When oi gets some way down t'road oi 'ears start awranglin' all over again, but oi don't think nuthin' much about it, an' goes 'ome ter me bed.'

'Did you recognize the man in the car,

Saunders?' asked the Coroner, as the old man stopped.

'Aye, sur, oi did,' replied old George, nodding vigorously.

'Is he in this Court?'

The old man's faded blue eyes travelled slowly over the rows of faces in front of him, and a hush fell on the crowded room. Suddenly his gaze became fixed, and he raised a gnarled hand.

'There 'e be, sur,' he said, pointing, 'that's 'im!'

A gasp broke from the throats of the expectant crowd, for he was pointing directly at Richard Tempest!

Trevor Lowe's lips compressed into a thin line. He was not surprised at the old man's identification, for he had seen in what direction the evidence was leading. He looked at Richard. His face was white and he was staring at old George Saunders as though he were a ghost. Near him Isabel Warren, with parted lips, stared too, in surprise and horror, her face pale and her hands clenched, so that the knuckles showed white under the stretched skin. The old man's evidence had evidently been a shock to her.

The Coroner's voice, as he began to further question old George, broke the dead silence, which had followed the old man's assertion. He put a number of questions to make sure that the old man had not made a mistake, and then dismissed him, recalling Richard Tempest.

Richard walked from his seat to the stand with a firm step, but the trembling of his hands belied his outward composure.

'Mr. Tempest,' said the Coroner, sternly, 'you have heard the evidence of the last witness. According to that evidence, at the time when you should have been in London, had the story you told us earlier been true, you were actually talking to your brother on the Minchester road, and not merely talking but quarrelling. What have you to say in explanation of this?'

Richard fumbled nervously with his tie before he answered.

'I admit that I was not speaking the truth when I said that I left at once for London after driving Roger to the Sheldons',' he said at length, in a voice that was scarcely audible. 'My — my financial position was desperate. I had that evening asked my brother for a loan, and he had refused. He'd never refused before, and I thought if I tried again I could persuade him.'

'Why did you try to conceal the fact that you had seen the deceased later that evening?' The Coroner's face was hard as he surveyed the nervous man before him.

'I didn't want it publicly known just how desperate my need for money was. If I'd said that I had seen Roger after he left the Sheldons' I should have had to explain why.'

'Instead of which you preferred to commit perjury,' said the Coroner sharply. 'Please remember that you are under oath, Mr. Tempest! Now we should like to hear the real facts.'

Richard, still pulling nervously at his tie, was silent. His general attitude was against him, and Lowe saw the jury glance significantly at each other.

'We are still waiting, Mr. Tempest,' said the Coroner, impatiently.

Richard passed the tip of his tongue

quickly across his dry lips.

'I knew that my brother would be leaving the Sheldons' about eleven,' he began dully, 'and I thought I would wait for him along the road and talk to him as I drove him the rest of the way home. He was surprised to see me, and not in the best of tempers. He wouldn't get in the car, saying that he preferred to walk, and this made me annoyed too. We started arguing, and, I'm afraid, we both completely lost our tempers in the finish. Finally I told him that he was unreasonable, and that he could keep his damned money.'

'What happened after that?' asked the Coroner, as the other stopped.

'I drove off. I went straight back to London.'

'And you left the deceased standing by the roadside, alive and well?'

'Yes.'

'You say your financial position was a desperate one. Is it not true that the death of your brother has made you a rich man?'

'I suppose so.'

'How long have you known that you

would inherit the bulk of his money?'

'I've always known it. He never made any secret of the fact.'

'Have you any income of your own?'

'A very small one, yes.'

'But not sufficient to enable you to live in the style you desired?'

'No, I'm afraid I'm rather of an extravagant nature.'

'So it would not be wrong to say that you depended mostly on what your brother gave you?'

'No, it would not be wrong to say that.'

'Thank you, Mr. Tempest. That is all I wish to ask you.'

Richard stepped heavily from the stand, and returned to his seat. His face was haggard, and Lowe guessed that he fully realised the unpleasantness of his position.

There were no other witnesses to call, and evidently the Coroner did not think it necessary to recall Inspector Mirren, for after a long perusal of his notes, and a preliminary cough, he began his summing up.

His speech was short, and Lowe, listening to it, could forecast the reactions of the jury almost for a certainty.

And his forecast proved right. Without leaving the box they held a hurried consultation, and the foreman rose.

'We find that the deceased met his death as the result of a knife wound inflicted by his brother, Richard Tempest,' he said.

'That is tantamount to a verdict of wilful murder against Richard Tempest,' said the Coroner. 'I agree with you entirely.'

The silence that followed was so pronounced that the sobbing gasp that escaped from the white lips of Isabel Warren was like the clap of thunder that presages a storm.

7

Surprise Item

That half strangled burst of sound impinging on the silence acted like a signal. Excited whispering broke out on all sides, and there was a scurry of feet as the pressmen made a dive for the exit and the nearest telephone.

The least, apparently, affected was the principal person concerned. Richard Tempest still sat in his seat, his face white, and a dazed expression in his eyes. It remained even when Inspector Mirren stepped to his side and quietly murmured the usual formula of arrest. Dully he got up and allowed himself to be led over to the two burly policemen who were waiting to take him to Minchester police station to be charged. Still in a daze, he walked between them to the street where a car was drawn up.

The police driver got down as they

approached, and opened the rear door, leaving the engine purring gently. Richard was propelled across the pavement and, suddenly, just as he had raised his foot to step into the machine his wits came back.

With the clearness of a searchlight cutting through the darkness of the night he realised just what was happening to him, and the knowledge sent a wave of panic breaking over him.

Acting on a sudden impulse, he charged the constable on his right with such force that the man went staggering across the pavement, swung half left, and planted a shattering blow on the second man's jaw. As he dropped with a grunt, Richard turned to deal with the driver, who had sprung forward to the assistance of his confreres. Flinging himself sideways, he shot out his left hand in a thrust that caught the man under the ear and sent him spinning like a top. Before he could recover his balance, Richard was in the car and behind the wheel. A click of gears, the roar of a violently accelerated engine, and he was away!

It had all happened so quickly that the

three police officers were still picking themselves up when Mirren, who had been detained by the Coroner, rushed out to see what the row was about.

His language, when he heard, was so violent, that an elderly lady who was passing scuttled away in horror and laid a complaint that afternoon to the local J.P.

When the first flood of his rage had ebbed, however, the Inspector realised that abusing his subordinates was not going to recapture his prisoner. He did the only thing he could do; since there was no car available to go in pursuit, he made for the nearest telephone, and within a few minutes an all-stations call had gone out with a description of the car and the wanted man.

He came back, still flushed with annoyance, to where Lowe, who had followed him out of the courtroom, was standing.

'Can you beat it?' he growled. 'The man we want dished up to us on a silver plate, and then these blithering numbskulls let him get away!'

The dramatist suppressed a desire to smile, for Mirren, in his anger, looked rather a harassed hen.

'You shouldn't have a great deal of difficulty in finding him again,' he said soothingly. 'In the meantime you can't do any more than you have, so why not come over to the Bull and have a drink? I want to talk to you.'

The inspector accepted the suggestion with alacrity, and when they were comfortably propped against the bar with a tankard of beer apiece, Lowe disclosed the reason for his invitation.

'I suppose,' he began quietly, 'you're convinced that Richard Tempest did kill his brother?'

Mirren paused with his tankard half way to his lips, and stared at him.

'Aren't you, sir?' he demanded.

The dramatist shook his head.

'No, I'm by no means convinced,' he declared.

'I don't think there's any doubt about it,' said Mirren, emphatically. 'He had the strongest possible motive. He was up to his neck in debt — there are writs out against him everywhere — I've been making inquiries — and his only hope to avoid a bust up was a loan from his brother. His brother refused, and he was desperate. The case against him is absolutely cut and dried, in my opinion.'

'Well, it's not in mine,' said Lowe. 'Look here, if he killed his brother as you suggest, why did he wait such a long time to do it? Why didn't he kill him that night when he waited for him on the Minchester road?'

'That point struck me too, sir,' replied the inspector, 'and I think I can explain it. I don't think the murder was premeditated. What I believe happened is this.' He took a deep draught of beer, wiped his lips, and proceeded: 'When Roger Tempest again refused Richard's plea for a loan, Richard lost his temper and there was a violent quarrel — we know that, he admitted it himself — and old George Saunders heard 'em. But I don't believe Richard's story as to how the quarrel ended. It's my opinion that in his rage he attacked his brother and laid him out. When he saw him unconscious, the idea came to him to keep him prisoner and force him to do what he wanted. He tried this, but Roger wouldn't give in. and then, as his financial affairs were daily becoming more pressing, he killed him, knowing that the money would come to him. How's that, sir?'

'It's ingenious, but not convincing,' answered the dramatist promptly. 'Your explanation makes out Richard to be a thoroughly callous, calculating scoundrel, and from what I've seen of him, I don't think he's anything of the kind. If he had killed his brother that night on the Minchester road in a fit of temper, I would agree it was possible, but even then I should say it was unlikely. That he would keep his brother a prisoner, and act in the way you assume he acted, is, to my mind, completely improbable.'

'Well, we shall see, sir,' grunted Mirren. 'Your arguments are a bit too deep for me. I prefer to deal in facts. If Richard Tempest is innocent, why did he bolt? That's not the action of an innocent man.'

'It's not necessarily the action of a guilty one,' retorted the dramatist. 'Richard Tempest possesses a definitely weak character, and, like all weak characters, he hates to face up to anything that is in the least unpleasant.'

Mirren scratched his chin thoughtfully, and slowly shook his head.

'I'm afraid I can't agree with you, sir,' he said. 'This fellow killed his brother right enough.' He swallowed the remainder of his beer, and set down the empty tankard. 'If you'll excuse me, Mr. Lowe,' he said, 'I must be off. There's going to be trouble over this chap getting away unless I can find him within the next few hours. Goodbye, sir.'

'Goodbye,' said Lowe, and when the inspector had gone, considered what he should do next. There was nothing to keep him in Long Dene, but he was feeling hungry, and he decided to have a late lunch at the Bull before returning to London.

It was a comfortable old inn, with a good dining room, and he found a vacant table beside one of the warped old diamond-paned windows. The place was fairly full, for a number of the people who had come to hear the inquest had apparently decided to lunch here, but he saw with thankfulness that they were all strangers. He had no wish to discuss the murder with any of the reporters, who would have considered his views a good scoop. No doubt they were all too busy following up the sensation of Richard Tempest's escape to find time for food.

He chose a grilled steak with care, but he was not destined to be allowed to eat it in peace, as he had hoped.

He was waiting for it to arrive, and filling in the time glancing through an old magazine, which he found on the window seat, when a voice at his side made him look up suddenly.

Isabel Warren was standing by the table looking nervously down at him.

8

The Lady in the Silver Fox

She greeted his look of surprise with a rather wan little smile.

'I'm so sorry to disturb you, Mr. Lowe,' she said, 'but I was anxious to see you before you returned to Town, and Inspector Mirren said you were in here.'

The dramatist got up and pulled out a chair.

'Please sit down, Miss Warren,' he said. 'You are not disturbing me at all. Perhaps you would care to join me?'

She shook her head as she took the chair he had offered.

'No, thank you,' she said. She looked a little ill-at-ease and uncomfortable.

'What was it you wished to see me about?' he asked, as she remained silent.

She hesitated, and then suddenly burst forth into a breathless explanation that mainly consisted of her repeated conviction that a dreadful mistake had been made, and that Richard was innocent of the crime of which he had been accused.

'He couldn't do a dreadful thing like that, Mr. Lowe!' she protested vehemently. 'It just isn't possible. The police have made a terrible mistake. Mr. Tempest was very fond of his brother; he would never have injured him.'

'I rather feel the same way,' admitted the dramatist. 'In fact, I said as much to Inspector Mirren a few minutes ago.'

'Did you?' she said, eagerly. 'Then that makes it so much easier for me to — I mean if you believe in Richard — in Mr. Tempest's innocence perhaps you would — ?' Her voice trailed away incoherently, and she stopped in confusion.

Lowe smiled.

'What you are trying to ask me,' he said gently, 'is whether I will try and prove that Richard Tempest is innocent of the charge which has been brought against him, isn't that it?'

'Yes,' she answered, 'that's what I want you to do. I — it's a lot to ask, but I should be so grateful if you — And you've been successful before — '

'I don't mind admitting to you, Miss Warren,' interrupted the dramatist, 'that I am intensely interested in this affair, and I shall be glad of the excuse, which your request has provided, to follow it up.'

She was overwhelming in her thanks, which he waved aside.

'Wait until I've done something before you thank me,' he said. 'You must remember that I can't guarantee any result.'

Before she left he arranged to call at the vicarage during the evening to meet her father, who had apparently been very fond of both Roger and Richard, and was much distressed at the death of the elder man.

'But the daughter is more distressed over the position of the younger,' thought Lowe, as he escorted the girl to the street. 'She may not realise it, but if that young lady isn't in love with that good-looking rascal I'm a Dutchman!'

He went back to the inn, found the proprietor, and booked two rooms. Then he put a call, through to his flat and spoke to his secretary.

'I want you to come down by the first available train,' he said, after he had briefly related the result of the inquest. 'I've taken rooms at the local pub, the Bull. You'd better come straight there. Oh, and by the way, you might bring a gun and some spare clips with the rest of the luggage. I don't anticipate having to use it, but you never know.'

'Right you are,' said Arnold White, cheerfully, 'I'll be there as soon as I can.'

Lowe phoned the police station at Minchester after his secretary had rung off, got on to Mirren, and told that harassed man the gist of his interview with Isabel.

'I'd like to work with you as much as possible,' he concluded.

'I'll give you all the assistance I can, sir,' said the Inspector, 'but I'm afraid you're only wasting your time. You know my opinion, and I think I'm right.'

'Well, that remains to be seen,' said the dramatist. 'I'm going to tackle this business from the point of view that Richard Tempest did not murder his brother.'

'If he didn't I should be glad to know who did, sir,' retorted Mirren.

'That's what I hope to find out!' said Lowe, and rang off. A little gentle exercise would do him good he decided, after being cooped up all the morning in the stuffy room where the inquest had been held, and went for a walk. He walked into Minchester, taking the same road that old George Saunders had traversed on the night when he had passed Roger Tempest and his brother, and heard them quarrelling.

Settling himself comfortably in the lounge he read the *Evening Comet,* which contained a verbatim report of the evidence. One point, which he had overlooked before, struck him as peculiar. In the evidence given by Hammerton, the literary agent had estimated Roger Tempest's fortune as comparative small to what it really was as revealed by Tempest's solicitor. And yet Hammerton had been in a position to know. The dead man's income had been entirely derived from his writing, and the receipts must have passed through the agent's hands. It was his business to collect all such monies, and, after deducting his ten per cent commission, pay the balance over to his client in such a way as he should instruct. Why, then, hadn't he been aware of the extent of Roger's wealth? The difference in the two estimates had been too large to be an accident, surely, Supposing it had not been an accident, supposing it had been a deliberately false statement? Was there any reason why Hammerton should do such a thing? The one that immediately leaped to mind was that the literary agent had been appropriating monies that didn't belong to him. But surely he couldn't have been such a fool. He would realise that he must be found out ... Was that why Roger Tempest had died? Had he realized that he was going to be found out and taken the only step that would prevent it?

Lowe frowned. He was allowing his imagination to run away with him. All this was pure supposition founded on one queer incident. There might be nothing in it at all. Still, it was worth thinking about. On previous occasions he had built up a chain of evidence on an even less substantial basis. If Hammerton had stolen money that didn't belong to him, it shouldn't be difficult to prove it. If everything was open and above board the money would be intact. The dramatist made a mental note to have a word with the dead man's lawyer at the first available opportunity.

He had reached this point in his cogitations when his attention was distracted by the arrival of a car at the door of the inn. At first he thought it was White, and then he saw through the window that the sole occupant of the rather blatant sports model was a woman, whose ensemble generally matched her rakish car. She was smoking a cigarette and titivating too artistically blonde hair in the driving mirror.

Presently she climbed out of the low seat and, swinging a silver fox fur by the middle, stalked into the lounge.

She gave him an appraising glance that held just the merest hint of an invitation as she passed, and a few seconds later he heard a high-pitched, and slightly nasal voice, demanding immediate attention from the management. The proprietor came hurrying from the rear regions a trifle breathlessly in response to the aged waiter's call.

'I want a room for the night,' said the lady with the silver fox, 'maybe for two nights.'

The proprietor was suitably helpful. He sent for his wife, and the guest was conducted upstairs. After a short lapse of time she came down and signed the register, which was produced for that purpose.

'You've been having some excitement here,' she said as she threw down the pen. 'I'll bet this murder has given this one-eyed dump a kick, eh?' She laughed a little harshly. 'Well, have my suitcase taken to my room, and get someone to put my car away.' She turned, and with another glance at Lowe, started to ascend the stairs again. Half way up she stopped and looked back at the gaping landlord.

'Oh, and you can send me up a double whiskey and soda,' she called, and disappeared round the bend.

Lowe got up slowly. Who was this

certainly attractive, but rather common woman? She was the last type one would expect to find in a village like Long Dene. He strolled over to the little table on which the register was kept, picked up the shabby book, and idly turned the pages. At length he came to the last entry, and the name he saw there, scrawled in thin, spidery writing sent him suddenly rigid.

The woman with the silver fox had signed herself 'Mrs. Roger Tempest'!

9

The Figure at the Window

Trevor Lowe stared down at the signature unable for the moment to believe his eyes.

Mrs. Roger Tempest!

It was a most unexpected and surprising development. It had been generally accepted that Roger Tempest was a bachelor. Hammerton had said so, and not even a hint that there might be a wife in the background had been dropped at the inquest. Even the dead man's solicitor apparently, then, had not known — or if he had, he had kept the knowledge to himself. Neither had this mysterious wife been mentioned in the will, for the lawyer would certainly have included her name when he had told the Coroner the names of those benefiting in Court.

This sudden appearance of a surprising Mrs. Tempest was a completely unlooked-for event, and the whole affair would have to be reconsidered in the fresh light that her advent shed. There might very well be something here that would supply a new angle to the murder. This woman was, apparently, a secret, which Roger Tempest had guarded well, since nobody had suspected her existence, and, if there was one secret in his life, there might very well be others.

The dramatist pursed his lips and rubbed gently at his chin. Did Isabel Warren know anything about this marriage, he wondered? She had been in the confidence of the dead man. He did not think she did, but he decided to ask her when he saw her that evening. Of course there was the possibility that the woman had no right to the name she had signed, She might just have done so for the sake of causing a sensation. There were curious mentalities like that.

He broke off in the midst of his thoughts as the aged waiter informed him that he was wanted on the telephone.

It was Inspector Mirren at the other end of the wire, and when he heard his voice, Lowe thought he was going to tell him that Richard had been caught. But though the Inspector's news concerned Richard, it was not of his arrest. The police-car had been found abandoned on the fringe of a wood, a little more than five miles beyond the village. A bicycle, belonging to a farmer's son, had been stolen near the same spot, and Mirren was of the opinion that the fugitive had taken it. Despite an intensive police search, however, there was no sign of either the bicycle or Richard.

It was on the tip of Lowe's tongue to tell the Inspector about the arrival of the woman calling herself Mrs. Tempest, but he refrained, deciding that he would wait until he had seen Isabel.

'I'll keep you posted if anything further turns up, sir,' promised the obliging Mirren and rang off.

Coming out of the room where the telephone was kept, the dramatist found that White had arrived. He took him up to his room, followed by the barman with the luggage, and waited while the secretary washed the dust of the journey from his face and hands. When he had freshened himself up he took him down to the vestibule and ensconced him at a little table in a secluded corner.

'Now we can talk,' he said, and proceeded to augment the meagre details, which he had been able to give over the telephone.

White listened with interest.

'It seems to be a queer affair,' he remarked, when his employer had finished. 'I'm not surprised that they brought in a verdict against this fellow, Richard.'

'Neither am I,' said Lowe. 'I expected it after the evidence of old George Saunders. But I don't think he's guilty, all the same.'

'Maybe this woman has got something to do with it,' said White, thoughtfully. 'It seems fishy that nobody knew anything about her before, and that now, directly Roger Tempest is dead, she should turn up openly.'

'That's exactly what I think,' agreed Lowe, 'and I want you to keep an eye on her, get acquainted with her if you can — I don't think you'll find it difficult — and see if she'll talk. I've got to go up to the Warrens', but I don't suppose I'll be late.'

He left White sitting in the vestibule, and set off for the vicarage at the end of the High Street. It was an old-fashioned house, standing in an acre or so of garden, and backed by the wooded hillside. There was an atmosphere of peace here that should not have been disturbed by even the smallest of worries, yet when the girl opened the door in answer to his knock, her face was drawn, and her eyes looked tired.

She greeted him with a smile, however, and invited him into the big hall.

'It's the maid's night off,' she said as she took his hat, 'so I'm deputising. Come into the lounge. Father's waiting anxiously to meet you. I'll let you into a secret, his hobby is reading detective stories! He's got stacks and stacks of them in his study.'

'And a very good hobby, too,' said Lowe, as he followed the girl into a large, pleasant room, with French windows that overlooked the old-world garden.

A short, squarely-built man rose to

greet him from a big comfortable-looking armchair. The Reverend Horatio Warren was a man in his early sixties, but there was a ruddy glow in his complexion, and a merry twinkle in his blue eyes that made him seem younger. He gripped the dramatist's hand with a strength that was surprising.

'This is a pleasure that I have been looking forward to ever since my daughter said that you were coming, Mr. Lowe,' he declared. 'Sit down, my dear sir, sit down.'

He waved the dramatist into a worn chair, and Lowe sat down with a murmured word of thanks.

'Now,' went on the little clergyman, his rosy, apple-like face beaming, 'what would you like in the way of refreshments? I can offer you some quite passable sherry or, if you would prefer it, a whiskey and soda.'

Lowe chose the sherry, and Isabel set the glasses down on a low Sheraton coffee table, and filled them from the decanter. When she had given one to Lowe, and one to her father, she took one herself and sat down on a large round pouffe between them.

The dramatist sipped the wine and expressed his appreciation.

'It is quite a good sherry, I believe,' said the vicar, 'although I am not an expert on such matters. It was a present from one of my parishioners.'

He produced a battered pipe and began to fill it.

'Don't hesitate to smoke, Mr. Lowe,' he said. 'I am, I fear, a slave to the nicotine habit.'

The dusk had fallen. The soft glow of the fading sunset filled the old garden with a rosy light that held a hint of the blue of the coming night. Trevor Lowe, taking advantage of the vicar's invitation, lit a cigarette, and leaned back in his chair.

'Would it surprise you to know that Roger Tempest was married?' he asked, quietly.

'It would surprise me very much,' said Isabel. 'What reason have you for suggesting such a thing, Mr. Lowe?'

'A — lady arrived late this afternoon at

the Bull,' he replied, 'and signed herself Mrs. Roger Tempest.'

It was dark now, and he could not see their faces, but he sensed their amazement and incredulity.

'It's impossible! There must be some mistake!' cried the vicar. 'I am certain that Roger was not married. He has lived in this village for over ten years, and he always confided in me. If he had been married, I cannot believe that he would not have told me.'

'I'm sure I should have seen or heard something about it, too,' said the girl, as she rose to light the lamps. 'I've dealt with all his private correspondence for the last two years, and I am sure I should have discovered if there had been a wife in the background.'

'Roger Tempest may have been at pains to keep his marriage a secret,' said Lowe. 'From what little I've seen of the lady she's nothing to boast about.'

He gave them a vivid and unvarnished description of the lady with the silver fox.

'She must be an impostor,' declared the vicar. 'Roger would never have married a woman like that — never!'

Lowe was not at all prepared to admit this. There was something undeniably attractive about the woman at the Bull that might quite easily have appealed to a very young man, and Roger had probably been very young when he had contracted the marriage. He kept this opinion to himself, however.

'Well, whether she is Mrs. Roger Tempest or not, can very easily be proved,' he said. 'There's little doubt that her reason for turning up like this immediately after the death of Roger is to see if there is any money going, and she'll have to produce a marriage certificate to prove her identity.'

'Even if she does, she'll be disappointed,' remarked Isabel; 'she wasn't mentioned in the will, according to the solicitor this morning.' She had lighted the three oil lamps, which was all the illumination the room boasted, and returned to her seat on the pouffe.

'Talking of solicitors,' said the dramatist, 'did Roger Tempest employ any other firm than the one represented at the inquest this morning?'

Isabel nodded.

'Yes,' she said, 'at least I don't know whether he employed another firm or not, but he dealt with one. A firm called Henkel and Witherstone of Clement's Inn. He used to write to them on the first of every month. He used to write himself, he never dictated that letter. But I remember the address because I used to post the letters with his others, and noted them in the stamp book.'

'The first of every month, eh?' muttered Lowe. 'It seems to me highly likely that these letters may have a direct connection with the mysterious Mrs. Tempest.'

'How?' asked the girl.

'Well,' he replied, 'he must have provided her with some sort of an allowance, and — ' He broke off as he saw her hand go suddenly up to her mouth, and her face whiten. A half strangled scream escaped her lips, and she stared fearfully at the window. He swung round quickly, and, for an instant, caught sight of a vague, shadowy figure, and a face peering in. The next second it was gone.

He sprang to his feet and dashed to the window. Heedless of the girl's alarmed protestations, he jerked back the catch and stepped out into the darkness. There was nobody to be seen. He heard a sound, however, away to his right, and raced off in that direction. A narrow path twisted away into the shadows of the garden, and he followed it. But he found no sign of the mysterious prowler, neither could he hear any sound of retreating footsteps, although he stopped once to listen.

He gave it up at last, and went back to the house. The vicar and Isabel were standing near the door as he came in the window, and he was struck by the change in their faces. It was only natural that they should have been startled by the appearance of the unknown marauder, but not to the extent that their faces betrayed. Here was an extremity of fear that was not warranted by the slight occurrence.

'There's nobody about,' said the dramatist, as he closed the windows. 'Did you recognise who it was?'

'No.' There was a queer rigidity in the

girl's voice as she answered him. 'No, I happened to look up while you were speaking, and saw a bearded face pressed against the glass, peering in. It — it startled me for a moment, that's all. I was foolish.'

'Probably a tramp, my dear,' muttered the vicar, shakily. 'They often come round here asking for food.' He took out his handkerchief and mopped his moist face. 'Dear me, it gave me quite a nasty turn.' He put away his handkerchief, then added: 'What about getting Mr. Lowe some supper, my dear?'

The girl nodded and moved over to the door, but the dramatist stopped her,

'If you don't mind, I don't think I'll wait,' he said, and they did not attempt to press him. In fact he had a curious conviction that they were glad he had curtailed his visit.

Going back to the inn he was very thoughtful. It was queer the sudden change that had come over those two. Why, if the figure at the window had been a tramp, as the vicar had suggested, had they both been so scared? And why had they shown even greater uneasiness when he had returned from his fruitless expedition into the garden? There was something here that wanted explaining, and he thought that the explanation might very well have a bearing on the mystery he was engaged in trying to solve.

10

The Man Who Died

Seated, on the morning following his visit to the vicarage, in the little lounge of the Bull Inn, Lowe thought over the whole affair, jotting down the leading points on a slip of paper on his knee. There were quite a number of things that he concluded were worth looking into. That discrepancy between the actual amount of the dead man's fortune and Mr. Hammerton's estimate; the circumstances in which Roger Tempest's marriage had taken place, and where and when; the possibility that in some obscure way his wife might benefit by his death.

He had just finished his notes, and had risen to his feet with the intention of seeking Arnold White, when a tall man came quickly into the vestibule, looked hurriedly round, and catching sight of Lowe, advanced with outstretched hand.

'Hello, Lowe, I heard you were staying here and I hoped I'd catch you in,' he said.

'My dear Gladwin,' said the dramatist, shaking the other's hand heartily. 'Of course, you live in this district. I'd forgotten that. How is your father?'

'He's dead.' The reply came in a voice that was not quite steady. 'He's dead, Lowe. He died suddenly during last night.'

The dramatist looked at the grief-stricken man before him, and his face was sympathetic.

'My dear fellow,' he said, 'I'm terribly sorry. What was the trouble? Heart?'

Malcolm Gladwin looked at him strangely as he shook his head.

'We don't know what it was,' he replied. 'The doctor refuses to give a certificate!'

Lowe raised his eyebrows.

'That's rather unusual,' he said. 'What reason does he give for refusing?'

'He says he is not satisfied as to the cause of death,' answered Gladwin. 'And I must admit the circumstances are rather mysterious.'

'In what way?' asked Lowe.

'Well, according to the doctor, the poor old guv'nor died from pneumonia, yet he was perfectly hale and hearty the day before, and in the best of health when he went to bed.'

The dramatist frowned. If the doctor hadn't made a mistake, it was certainly strange. Pneumonia does not reach an acute stage in a few hours, without any previous symptoms of its presence. It was true that Sir Horace Gladwin had been an old man, but, even so, a disease like pneumonia would have to run its normal course. It was very unlikely that it could be contracted and prove fatal in so short a time.

'I'm not surprised that your doctor refuses to give a certificate in the circum-stances,' he said, after a moment's pause. 'In which case, of course there will have to be an inquest.' The other nodded.

'That's what Doctor Bently says,' he replied. 'He says he refuses to take the responsibility.' He stopped and fingered his chin nervously. 'Look here, Lowe,' he went on suddenly, 'I don't believe that father's death was natural!'

The dramatist looked at him quickly.

'How do you mean, exactly?' he asked. 'Do you mean that you suspect foul play?'

'I don't quite know what I mean,' answered Malcolm wearily. 'But father hasn't been himself for some weeks. There's been something bothering him — something on his mind . . . '

'Are you suggesting that your father committed suicide?' said Lowe, quietly, as he paused and hesitated.

'I don't know what to think, but there's something queer somewhere, and I wish you'd look into it. That's why I came along to see you.' Malcolm passed a hand over his smooth hair, and his eyes were troubled as they met Lowe's. 'I thought, perhaps, you might have a word with the doctor. The guv'nor and you were pretty good friends and — well, I'd feel more satisfied if you would just take a look at things.'

Lowe hesitated before replying. At the present moment he had all his work cut out with the Tempest murder, but, as the other had said, he and old Sir Horace had known each other for a good many years, and he had spent several enjoyable weekends at the big, rambling, old house near Minchester. It seemed churlish to refuse the young man's request, and there was something definitely queer about the old man's death.

He came to a decision after a few seconds' consideration.

'All right, Malcolm,' he said, 'I'll look into it for you. We'll go along to Abbey Lodge now, if you like.'

'I'm damned grateful, Lowe,' said Gladwin, his eyes lighting up. 'It's relieved my mind no end. If there is anything wrong — and I'm sure there is — you're bound to spot it.'

'Well, I'm not so sure about that,' said the dramatist, 'but I'll do my best. Just one minute while I have a word with my secretary, and I'll be with you.'

He hurried up the stairs and found White in his room. Rapidly he explained what had happened to that interested young man.

'I don't suppose I shall be very long,' he concluded, 'it looks very much like a case of suicide to me, though why old Sir

Horace should take his life I don't know. Anyway, while I'm gone you stop here and keep an eye on our lady friend. If she goes out follow her, and note where she goes and whom she sees. I'll get back as soon as I can.'

He rejoined Malcolm in the vestibule, and just as they were preparing to leave a man came quickly into the inn, shot Lowe an embarrassed glance, and hurried into the bar.

It was Bruce Hammerton!

The dramatist's thoughts were busy as he took his place beside Malcolm in the latter's car. What was the literary agent doing in Long Dene? And what was he doing at the Bull? There had been something furtive about his manner that seemed to Lowe a little suspicious. There was no reason why he should have looked so embarrassed if his visit to the Bull was quite open and above board. And then it suddenly struck the dramatist why he was there. He had come to see Mrs. Tempest!

Lowe's brows drew down over his eyes. If that was the case there was something between them, and already he was a trifle suspicious of the stout Mr. Hammerton. That business of the discrepancy . . .

He turned the matter over in his mind during the short journey to Abbey Lodge, and he was still thinking about it when they reached their destination.

An imposing mansion of mellow brick, Abbey Lodge had been the home of the Gladwin family for generations. It stood in something over eighty acres of parkland just outside the market town of Minchester, and a distance of four miles from Long Dene.

As the car came to a halt on the wide gravel sweep before the front door, the massive portal was opened by a soberly-clad servant.

'Any message, Ward?' asked Malcolm, as the man took their hats.

'Yes, sir,' answered the servant, 'Dr. Bently called again. When he found you were out he said he would call back in about an hour.'

Malcolm nodded and led his friend into the library.

'I'm glad Bently's coming back,' he said. 'You'll be able to have a word with him. He'll probably be more communicative to you than to me. You see, he's been our doctor for years, and he will treat me as if I was a kid. Now what would you like to do first?'

'I think I had better take a look at the body,' answered Lowe. 'Shall we go upstairs?'

'Yes.' Malcolm crossed to the door at once. 'As the discovery was only made this morning, nothing has been touched, and I locked the door of the guv'nor's bedroom before I came over to see you.'

Lowe followed him up the wide staircase in silence. When the door was unlocked the dramatist stood for a second on the threshold allowing his eyes to travel slowly round the room. It was very little changed from when he had last seen it. There were the bookshelves with Sir Horace's favourite books, mostly biographies and books of travel. There was the deep leather chair drawn up near the fireplace and the flat-topped writing table at right angles to the source of light. There were the prints and photographs, and the faded old Persian rugs that covered the polished floor. Nothing was altered, nothing had changed — except the still and silent figure on the bed, the outlines of which could be seen so clearly beneath the white sheet that covered it.

Without a word, he went over and reverently drew away the covering from the face of the dead man. The features were set and curiously congested, as though in his last extremity he had fought desperately for breath. Lowe pursed his lips, and looked up at Malcolm.

'How was he found?' he whispered. 'I mean did it look as though he had died peacefully?'

'No,' was the low-voiced reply, 'the bedclothes were disordered, and he was lying half out of bed, with one arm thrown across that table.'

He nodded towards a small bedside table that contained two or three books and a partly burned candle in a tall candlestick.

'In fact he had knocked the candle over,' went on Malcolm. 'I picked it up off the floor.'

'H'm,' murmured Lowe, looking at it,

'presumably the candle was alight when it was knocked over, and falling onto the floor put it out. You can see that by the way the soft wax has been pressed over the wick. Did your father always read in bed by candlelight?'

'Yes,' answered the other, 'always. Poor old dad was one of the old school, you know. He hated anything modern. Most of his life he'd gone to bed by candlelight, and he liked to remember those times. I used to tell him that it was bad for his eyes, for he always read for an hour or two before going to sleep, but he wouldn't listen. He had been reading last night. The book was open on the bed when he was found.'

'I see,' Lowe nodded absently, his eyes roving over the bed and the table near its head. 'Then if that candle was a new one when it was lighted, your father must have been reading for about two hours before — well, before whatever happened.'

He stooped suddenly, and peered down at the surface of the bedside table.

Malcolm saw his face go rigid, and his lips set.

'What is it?' he asked quickly. 'What have you found?'

'Something very extraordinary and very significant,' replied the dramatist. 'Look here.'

Malcolm came to his side, and saw that on the tabletop lay three dead flies.

'How did they die?' muttered Lowe, speaking almost to himself. 'They are not singed, so they didn't get burned in the flame of the candle. The candle! I wonder — '

He picked it up and examined it. After a moment or two he sniffed at it gingerly, frowned and put it down again.

'Well,' began Malcolm eagerly, 'have you found anything?'

'I don't know.' Lowe caressed his chin thoughtfully. 'I don't know. Did you notice a peculiar smell in this room this morning — like rotting vegetables?'

'Why, yes, there was something of the sort,' said Malcolm. 'What — '

'It's quite strong about that candle,' said Lowe before he could finish. 'It may not be anything. Something, perhaps in the colouring matter. On the other hand there are those dead flies . . . ' He broke off and picked up the candlestick again. 'Tell me,' he went on quickly, 'did your father always use green candles? This kind is more usually used for decorative purposes than for illumination.'

'Now you come to mention it,' said Malcolm, 'he didn't. He always used the plain white kind. I've never seen a candle like that in the house before.'

The dramatist's eyes gleamed suddenly.

'Three dead flies and a green candle that has a queer smell,' he muttered. 'Is there any connection? Malcolm, I believe there has been a very cunning crime committed, and I think your doctor was acting wisely when he refused to sign a death certificate!'

11

The Sample

Malcolm Gladwin stared at his friend in horrified consternation.

'Good God!' he breathed. 'You're not suggesting that the guv'nor was murdered?'

Lowe looked at him steadily.

'I am,' he answered. 'But I'm only suggesting it mind. I have no proof yet.'

'I knew there was something wrong,' muttered the young man, huskily. 'I knew that he hadn't died naturally, but murder — '

'Before we go into that,' said Lowe, 'we'll make certain that someone wanted to kill him. Can I have a word with your servants?'

'Do anything you like, old man!' replied Malcolm, 'only get to the bottom of this dreadful business! If the guv'nor was murdered I'll never rest until I've caught the brute who did it.'

They went down to the library, and Lowe brought the candle with him. At his request Malcolm sent for the butler, Ward.

'Now, Ward,' said the dramatist, when the man arrived, 'I want to ask you a few questions. First, do you know if the stock of candles which Sir Horace habitually used has run out?'

The butler looked rather surprised, and shook his head.

'No, sir,' he answered at once. 'The month's supply only arrived a few days ago.'

'Next,' said Lowe, 'have you any candles like this in the house?'

Ward peered at the half-used candle and shook his head again.

'No, sir,' he said. 'To my knowledge there are no candles like that in the house, nor have there ever been any.'

'Can you suggest, then, how this came to be in the candlestick in Sir Horace's bedroom?'

'No, sir.'

'Would any of the maids have put it there?'

'I should very much doubt it, sir,' said the butler. 'I don't think they would do such a thing without consulting me. Apart from which, sir, where would they get it from?'

'These candles are not difficult to obtain, perhaps one of the servants brought one in with her?'

The butler's expression was dubious.

'Perhaps you would like to ask them yourself, sir?' he suggested, and Lowe agreed that he would.

The three maids came, looking a little scared and were questioned. But none of them had seen the green candle before or knew anything about it.

'It would appear as though it was your father himself who brought it into the house,' said Lowe, when the servants had been dismissed.

Malcolm frowned.

'It certainly looks like it,' he agreed, 'but I can't see what for.'

He broke off as there came a sharp rat-tat-tat-tat from the hall.

'That's Bently, I expect,' he said, and he was right, for a few seconds later the doctor was announced.

He was a fussy, bird-like, little man, with white hair, and a pair of shrewd eyes that appeared to miss nothing. He wore a pair of pince-nez glasses on the end of a broad ribbon, which had a habit of continually falling off the bridge of his nose while he was talking.

'Ah! H'm, Mr. Lowe,' he snapped in a high-pitched voice, when the dramatist was introduced. 'I'm very glad to make your acquaintance, sir. Very glad indeed. I think you are likely to find this a very interesting case, sir.'

'You are, I understand, unable to state the cause of Sir Horace's death?' said Lowe.

'You understand rightly, sir,' replied Doctor Bently bluntly. 'I am quite unable to account for it. I have been attending Sir Horace for a slight foot trouble recently and visited him last only three days ago. I wish to emphasise the fact, sir, that apart from that little disability his health was as sound as ever a man's could be. The next I hear is that he is dead! He had died suddenly during the night, and the only symptoms I can find are those of pneumonia. It is ridiculous, sir, completely ridiculous! The man could not have contracted pneumonia in the time. I positively refuse to sign a certificate of death until I am convinced of the cause.'

He clapped his glasses on his nose and glared from one to the other, upon which they immediately fell off and he caught them deftly.

'Could you say whether death was instantaneous or not?' asked the dramatist.

'It was not instantaneous,' answered Doctor Bently, promptly. 'I should say there was suffocation, which caused convulsions.'

'That was my opinion,' said Lowe. 'Well, perhaps the post-mortem will reveal the cause.' He turned to Malcolm. 'Can you find me a piece of brown paper and some string?' he asked.

'There's usually some in the drawer of that table,' replied Malcolm, nodding toward a large mahogany table, containing papers and magazines, close to where the dramatist was standing. He started to move across, but Lowe had already pulled open the long drawer. It was full of odds and ends of string and wrapping paper, evidently carefully preserved from various parcels, and the dramatist was searching for something suitable to wrap up the candle and stick when he came on a shallow box. With it was a crumpled letter, and he would have passed it by if, on one corner, he had not seen the word 'Candle' in printed letters.

With sudden interest he took the paper out of the drawer and smoothed it out. What he had seen was part of the name of a firm — 'The Gloworm Candle Co., Ltd.' — and the paper was a typed letter. A quick glance showed him that it was addressed to Sir Horace.

'Dear Sir,

'We have heard from our local retailer that you are a regular user of our candles, and we would like to draw your attention to a new candle which we are putting on the market. It is, in our opinion, infinitely superior to anything we have manufactured before.

It burns longer, with a steadier flame, and gives a much more brilliant light, although the price is the same as our standard product. We enclose a free sample, and we venture to predict that when you have tried it you will use no other candle.'

The letter was signed, 'C. A. Gleeson, General Sales Manager.'

Lowe pursed his lips. Here was a perfectly simple explanation for the presence of the candle. Sir Horace had decided to test its properties, and had used it in place of one of the stock of candles in the house. Probably the peculiar odour which he had noticed attached to it was due to some special ingredient in the manufacture. Altogether it looked as though the candle was quite innocuous after all. Still there were those dead flies to be accounted for . . .

He showed the letter to Malcolm.

'That seems to account for the candle,' he said.

Malcolm read it and wrinkled his forehead.

'I've never seen this before,' he said. 'In the drawer was it? I suppose Dad must have shoved it there with the wrapping. Well, this looks as though your idea about the candle was wrong.'

'It does,' admitted the dramatist. 'And yet — '

'What's all this about a candle?' broke in the little doctor, glancing from one to the other rapidly, and Lowe explained.

'It's queer about the flies. I never noticed 'em,' said Doctor Bently, frowning. 'But the candle couldn't have had anything to do with it obviously.'

'Unless,' remarked Lowe, 'something got into it by accident during the manufacture. That's not impossible. There must be a reason for those dead flies, doctor.'

'Well, the analyst will be able to tell you if there is anything other than ordinary wax,' said Bently. 'I must be going. They'll be sending for the body, Malcolm, during the day, in order to make the post-mortem. I'll attend to all the details, you needn't worry at all. Goodbye, my boy, goodbye, Mr. Lowe, I shall be seeing you again, of course.'

'If you will wait just a moment while I pack this candle up,' said the dramatist, 'I'll come with you. There's nothing more I can do here, at present.'

He made a neat parcel of the candle and stick, took his leave of Malcolm, and accompanied the little doctor to his car.

'Can I drop you anywhere?' asked Bently.

'Yes, if you happen to be going anywhere near the Bull,' answered Lowe.

'I wasn't, but I can!' grunted the other. 'Jump in!'

Arnold White was sitting rather gloomily in the little lounge when Lowe got back.

'Well, what was it? A mare's nest?' he asked, as his employer joined him.

Lowe shook his head.

'I think there is something very wrong indeed,' answered Lowe, gravely, and proceeded to relate what he had discovered.

White listened with interest.

'It certainly sounds odd,' he agreed.

'I'm going to take the candle up to Professor Van Wyck this afternoon and get him to see if there is anything wrong with it,' said the dramatist. 'If there isn't, well, then that's that. If there is, I shall go and see these candle people and try and discover how the foreign substance got in.'

White looked serious.

'If some sort of poison got into those candles at the factory,' he said, 'and they have sent out a number of these samples, there might be an epidemic of deaths.'

Lowe nodded.

'That's what I'm thinking of,' he said. 'And that's why I want to act quickly. I shan't wait for lunch, I'll have some when I get to town, but I shall be back for dinner. In the meanwhile you had better hang around here. Have you seen anything of Mrs. Tempest this morning, by the way?'

'No,' answered the secretary, 'but that fellow Hammerton has.'

'Oh,' muttered Lowe, swiftly, 'so he did come to see her?'

'Yes, he went up to her room almost directly after you'd gone,' replied White. 'I heard him ask the waiter. But he wasn't there long. He left in about ten minutes, and looked pretty bad tempered too.'

'I'd like to know what passed between them during that ten minutes,' said Lowe, thoughtfully. 'This friendliness between Roger Tempest's mysterious wife and his literary agent strikes me as rather suspicious.'

'He didn't look very friendly when he left,' said White. 'He looked as though he'd had a good dressing down.'

'We shall have to inquire more deeply into that gentleman's activities,' said Lowe. 'I'm inclined to believe that he and the lady, between them, may know a lot more about the death of Roger Tempest than they should.'

He rose to his feet.

'Well,' he said, 'I must leave you to look after the Tempest affair for the moment, while I try and clear up this business of the green candle. It's rather a nuisance that it should have happened just now, but it can't be helped. I promised Malcolm that I would do what I could, and I will.'

12

Di-phosgene!

Professor Van Wyck lived at Hammer-smith in an old-fashioned house that backed on to the river. He was a gigantic man with a tiny wisp of beard, that looked a trifle absurd on such a vast face, and a great mop of greyish-brown hair.

He greeted Lowe effusively, and led him into an incredibly untidy room, lined with books and littered with papers.

'Now,' he roared in a voice that was like a foghorn with asthma, 'what do you want? You never come to see me unless you want something, so what is it?'

The dramatist told his story, and produced the candle.

Van Wyck took it, sniffed at it, and his eyes narrowed.

'Come into the lab.,' he boomed briefly, and lumbered over to a door which stood partly open. The room beyond was lofty with a skylight — it had at one time been a studio — and surrounded with shelves containing countless bottles of every conceivable shape and size. A long, acid-stained bench ran down one side, under the window, covered with a jumble of retorts and scientific instruments.

'Sit down,' said Van Wyck, waving a huge hand towards a chair. 'I'll let you have the verdict in a few minutes.'

He strode over to the bench, dragged up a chair, and sat down.

For some time there was no sound except the chinking of glass against glass, and the heavy breathing of the scientist. Then suddenly Van Wyck swung round.

'Well, here's your answer,' he roared. 'Di-phosgene! There's been some filthy work somewhere, Lowe! A capsule of di-phosgene, which is a pretty deadly gas, was inserted in this candle near the wick. When the flame reached it the gas was released, and that's what killed those flies and the old man. A filthy trick on somebody's part! He wouldn't notice anything for a time, and then he'd find it difficult to breathe. Probably he tried to get out of bed, and that was fatal. Had he kept quiet and called for help, he might have saved himself. It's a peculiarity of di-phosgene that it is any sudden exertion after the gas has been inhaled that causes death. What really happens is that the victim is literally drowned in his own blood, hence the symptoms are similar to pneumonia. I don't think there is any doubt that this was a deliberately planned murder!'

The dramatist was not really surprised at the verdict. He had had a feeling that accident had not been responsible for his old friend's death, although he had, naturally, to take such a possibility into account. It was possible, though hardly probable, that some kind of poison had got into the candle during manufacture, but scarcely nature, or in the form that had been discovered by Van Wyck. The fact that a capsule of di-phosgene had been used, almost eliminated the possibility of accident, and left the only alternative — murder. For it was inconceivable to suppose that if Sir Horace had intended to take his own life he would have adopted such an elaborate means.

There was, however, still that faint chance of accident to be investigated, and Lowe decided, when he left Van Wyck, to put the matter finally to the test.

The Gloworm Candle Co. had their offices and factory at Croydon. It was a large modern building, and the dramatist went in the main entrance, and inquired for Mr. Gleeson, the sales manager. The commissionaire, to whom he put the inquiry, looked at him blankly, and asked him to repeat the name.

Lowe did so, and the man shook his head.

'No one of that name here, sir,' he said positively. 'Are you sure you've got the right name?'

'I thought I had,' said the dramatist. 'What is the name of your sales manager?'

'Mr. Stephen Parker, sir,' replied the commissionaire.

'Very well then, I'd better see him,' said Lowe.

The commissionaire ambled away, spoke for a moment on the telephone in his office, and returned.

'Will you come this way, sir?' he said, and led the way over to the lift.

Lowe was wafted up two floors, and deposited in a long corridor, with doors at intervals down one side, and a window at either end.

Mr. Parker's room was at the extreme end. It was a very clean room, with a very clean desk, and Mr. Parker was a very clean man.

Lowe came to the point at once. Briefly, without going into unnecessary details, he explained the reason for his visit, concluding by showing the sales manager the letter.

Mr. Parker was obviously nonplussed. He looked at it, read it, read it again, and stared at the dramatist blankly.

'This letter couldn't have come from us,' he said, shaking his head. 'We have no new candle on the market, and in any case we should not adopt this procedure. It is entirely out of keeping with our policy. I can't understand it at all.'

'Then you know nothing about that letter or the sample to which it refers?' said Lowe.

'Nothing at all,' declared the sales manager. 'It never came from this firm. There's no one of the name of Gleeson here, and there never has been.'

'But that is written on a sheet of your firm's paper?' said the dramatist, and Mr. Parker nodded.

'Oh, yes, it's our paper,' he answered frowning. 'I can't understand it at all.'

'Would it be possible for anybody to get hold of a sheet of your headed paper — any stranger, I mean?' asked Lowe.

'It would,' said Mr. Parker. 'There is a supply in the waiting room downstairs. Anyone could help themselves if they wanted to.'

'Then that, apparently, is what must have happened,' said the dramatist. 'I'm much obliged for your information. It has been of considerable help.'

He shook hands with the worried Mr. Parker, assured him that no trouble would accrue to his firm, and left the building.

Driving back to Long Dene he was very thoughtful and grave. He found the Inspector sitting gloomily in his little office, and without preamble told him what he had learned.

Mirren listened with startled surprise.

'Good Lord!' he exclaimed, when Lowe had finished. 'Things are getting pretty hot round here! First Mr. Tempest, and now Sir Horace. I'm very grateful, Mr. Lowe, for what you have done, and of course I'll look into the matter at once. I shall have to see the Chief Constable immediately.'

'Any news of Richard Tempest?' asked the dramatist.

Mirren shook his head despondently.

'Not a smell of him,' he declared. 'The earth might have swallowed him up! He's completely vanished. If I don't find him soon the Chief Constable'll insist on calling in the Yard, and that won't do me any good.'

Lowe left him the centre of a deep depression and went back to the Bull. White was waiting dinner for him, and after a wash, he joined the secretary in the dining room.

'Well,' said Arnold, 'did you find out anything?'

'Quite a lot,' answered Lowe, 'but I'm not going to talk about it now. I'll tell you later.'

He did so when, after the meal was over, they strolled towards the vicarage.

White made no comment until he had finished, and then he whistled

'What a cunning scheme,' he said. 'I wonder who the bright person was who thought that out.'

'I should like to know that,' said Lowe, grimly.

He turned in at the vicarage gate as he finished. The Warrens were not expecting him that evening, but the vicar had known Sir Horace, and Lowe thought it was just possible that he might supply some useful information.

Isabel answered the door, and appeared a little startled to see them.

'Come in Mr. Lowe,' she said, after a momentary hesitation. 'Father's busy just at present, so would you mind waiting in the dining room for a little while, and I'll go and tell him you're here?'

She ushered them into the big, old-fashioned room and hurried away.

Lowe frowned slightly. There was something a little peculiar in the girl's manner. She had seemed a trifle embarrassed, for some reason. Perhaps they had chosen an inopportune moment for their call. He could hear the faint hum of voices, and presently a door shut somewhere. A few seconds later Isabel returned. She was smiling cheerfully now as she escorted them into the comfortable lounge where Lowe had sat before. Most likely, he thought, the vicar had had a visitor. Someone from the parish who had gone.

He introduced Arnold White, and the clergyman gave him a hearty welcome, but there was something in the atmosphere that had not been there when Lowe had paid his previous visit. It was too vague to be definitely catalogued; a trace of constraint, mingled with a hint of uneasiness.

'Well,' said the vicar, when they had been given chairs and declined the offer of refreshment, 'what are the latest developments, Mr. Lowe?'

'So far as the Tempest business goes,' replied the dramatist, 'there aren't any.

Richard seems to have completely disappeared, and, at the moment, things
remain very much as they were. I'm afraid
that I haven't been able to do much today
in the matter. I daresay you've heard of
Sir Horace Gladwin's sudden death?'

The old man nodded.

'Yes,' he said, 'and a great shock it was
to me. I hear that there is some doubt as
to the cause of death too?'

'There was,' said the dramatist, a little
grimly, 'but there is none now. I'm afraid
that Sir Horace was murdered.'

The vicar uttered a horrified exclamation.

'Good gracious, Mr. Lowe, you can't
mean that!' he said. 'Surely there must be
some mistake . . . '

'There is no mistake,' replied Lowe,
shaking his head. 'When the doctor
refused the certificate, young Gladwin
asked me to look into the matter, and I've
spent the entire day doing so. The result is
that I have proved, beyond reasonable
doubt, that Sir Horace was murdered.'

'You horrify me,' said the old clergyman. 'Really I can scarcely believe it

possible. Sir Horace was greatly liked in the neighbourhood. Who could have wanted to harm him?'

'That I can't tell you,' replied the dramatist, 'but somebody did, and succeeded.'

'How was he killed?' asked the girl in a low voice, speaking for the first time.

'In a particularly ingenious manner,' answered Lowe, and related the result of his inquiries.

'Amazing!' muttered the vicar, when he had heard the story of the candle. 'A fiendish plan, but certainly clever . . . What is it, my dear?'

He broke off and looked at his daughter. She had started to speak and stopped.

'I don't know,' she said, her brows drawn down over her eyes, 'but what Mr. Lowe has been telling us seems somehow familiar to me. It — it sounds silly, I know, but I seem to have heard it all before!'

Lowe, a sudden light of interest in his eyes, leaned forward.

'Do you mean, Miss Warren,' he said, 'that you have heard of someone else being killed in the same way?'

'Well, yes, something of the sort,' said

the girl, still with that puzzled look on her face. 'And yet not quite that. I — I can't explain exactly . . . '

'Perhaps,' suggested her father, 'you have read of a similar crime. I must confess that it appears to me more like fiction than real life . . . '

'Yes, that's it!' cried the girl, suddenly jumping to her feet. 'It was fiction!' A strange, startled, expression came into her face. 'It was fiction! The murder that actually happened — the murder that Mr. Lowe has been telling us about, is identical in every detail with the plot of a new novel which Roger Tempest planned some months before he — before he was killed!'

13

A New Angle

Trevor Lowe stared at the girl in genuine surprise. This was something he had not expected. Up to this moment the two crimes had appeared to be entirely separate, but now here was a definite link that had presented itself in the most unexpected manner.

'This is really most extraordinary, Miss Warren,' he said. 'You are quite certain of what you say?'

'Quite,' she answered. 'It was stupid of me not to remember it at once.'

'Is there any record of this plot in existence?' asked the dramatist, and she nodded.

'Yes,' she said. 'I made quite a number of notes at Mr. Tempest's dictation. They will be with the rest of his papers at the White House.'

'I should like to see those notes at the

first available opportunity,' said Lowe. 'This may be very important. It certainly establishes a connection between these two crimes, though ... ' He stopped suddenly as there came a swift step on the gravel path outside the open french windows. A shadow fell across the ray of light that streamed out from the room. and Isabel uttered a little startled gasp. And then a cheerful voice boomed out, breaking the momentary tenseness, and a jovial figure loomed into the light.

It was Mr. Sheldon.

'Hello, people!' he cried brightly, as he stepped into the room. 'Hope I didn't startle you.'

The girl gave a sigh of relief, and the vicar, who had started half out of his chair, sank back again, puffing out his cheeks as the pent-up air escaped from his lungs.

The architect chuckled as he saw the effect his unexpected appearance had caused.

'I seem to have created a stir,' he remarked. 'Sorry, very sorry!'

The vicar looked a little vexed.

'Well, really, Sheldon,' he said, 'you

might have used a little more discretion. Your sudden appearance was rather startling. Why on earth didn't you come to the front door, my dear fellow?'

Sheldon instantly became apologetic.

'I really am most frightfully sorry,' he said. 'I suppose I should have done. But I saw the light in this room and the window open, and I thought I'd just walk in. How are you, Mr. Lowe? I always seem to time my visits when you are here.'

The dramatist smiled.

'I'm afraid that is not entirely your fault, Mr. Sheldon,' he replied pleasantly. 'I have been making myself rather a nuisance, here, lately.'

'Well, well,' said Sheldon good-humouredly, 'if you're having a conference, don't let me interrupt. I only came to have a word with the vicar, as I had to postpone my appointment with him this morning. But — '

'I suppose you're anxious to get those details settled concerning the fête?' broke in the vicar. 'I shall be glad to get them off my mind too. If Mr. Lowe will excuse us, we can go into my study and discuss them.'

Lowe rose to his feet.

'White and I will have to be going, anyway,' he said. 'So I'll say goodbye!'

The vicar shook hands, and carried the beaming Mr. Sheldon off to his study.

'Well, good night, Miss Warren,' said the dramatist. 'If it will be convenient to you, I should like you to accompany me to the White House in the morning and collect those notes.'

He arranged to meet her at ten o'clock, and they took their leave. As they walked slowly back to the Bull, Lowe was silent thinking over this latest and most surprising development, and Arnold White, who was bursting to discuss it, had to possess his soul in patience.

The landlord was in the lounge when they entered the inn, and after a remark about the weather, Lowe put a tactful question regarding Mrs. Tempest. To his surprise the landlord told him that she had left a short while before in her car. A gentleman had called for her, had paid her bill, and they had driven off together. From the landlord's description the dramatist had no difficulty in recognising

Bruce Hammerton!

Here was another mysterious factor in the tangle. Just what was the connection between Hammerton and Mrs. Tempest? Had the literary agent known her long, or did the acquaintance date from his previous visit? Lowe was inclined to think that it was of longer duration. He made up his mind to call on Messrs. Henkel and Witherstone during the course of the following day and see what information, if any, they could give him concerning Mrs. Tempest.

He awoke the next morning to find that the weather had changed. Grey clouds scudded across a lowering sky, driven before a chill wind, and although it was not raining, rain was not far off. As he dressed, Lowe remembered his appointment with Isabel Warren but a shock was in store for him. Coming down the stairs he met the landlord in the vestibule. The man looked excited, and when he saw the dramatist his excitement broke into speech.

'Have you heard the news, sir?' he said. 'About Mr. Tempest's place.'

'The White House, do you mean?' snapped Lowe.

'Yes, sir,' answered the landlord. 'It caught fire during the night. I've just heard — '

But Lowe was already out of the door. Hurrying round to the stables, which had been converted into a garage, he got out his car and went speeding through the village towards the Minchester road.

The White House stood among a screen of trees, but he could see the smoke that was swirling up into the leaden sky, long before he reached the house itself. Apparently all Long Dene had turned out to watch the spectacle. The roadway was crowded with people, and several cars had been parked under the tall hedges. The first person to greet him as he brought his own car to stop was the Reverend Horatio Warren. The little clergyman was very excited, and poured out the story of the fire in a volume of stumbling words.

The alarm had been given by Stiller. He had woken about five o'clock in the morning, gasping for breath, to find his room full of smoke. Staggering out onto the landing he had discovered that the staircase was already burning furiously. He had managed luckily to get out of the window of his room, drop to the balcony below, and from thence to the ground. The whole of the ground floor was ablaze, and seeing that he could do nothing on his own he had taken his bicycle from the outhouse and ridden to the vicarage, where he had telephoned the police. They, and the local fire brigade, had hurried to the spot, and, with the help of some labourers, had succeeded in getting quite a lot of the furniture from the downstairs rooms onto the lawn before the fury of the fire stopped any further salvage work. The house itself was doomed. It was very old and had contained a lot of timber. When Lowe saw it, it was still smouldering — a heap of blackened stone and brick.

Inspector Mirren was surveying the depressing sight, when the dramatist accompanied the vicar up the short drive to get a closer view, and he turned as they joined him.

'This is a queer business, sir,' he said.

'There seems to be no reason at all why the place should have caught fire. Stiller says that there were no fires in the house at all, and he doesn't smoke, so it couldn't have been that. I can only put it down to a fused electric wire.'

'Perhaps that was it,' said Lowe, though he had little doubt in his own mind that the fire had been started deliberately. 'Where did it start, does Stiller know?'

'Yes,' answered Mirren, 'he says that it must have started in the study, but I don't see how that can have been right because the room has been locked up ever since the murder.'

'It's a great shame,' said the vicar, shaking his head sorrowfully. 'Such a charming house.'

'Yes, it's a great shame,' agreed the dramatist, but he was not referring to the house. He was thinking of those notes for Roger Tempest's novel that were now nothing more than scattered tinder. This fire was no accident. Of that he was convinced. It had been a deliberate act on someone's part, carried out with the object of destroying that piece of possible evidence.

'Good morning, Mr. Lowe. This is terrible isn't it?' Isabel's voice broke in on his thoughts, and turning, he found the girl at his side.

'It is certainly very unfortunate, Miss Warren,' he said gravely, and something in his tone brought a startled expression to her face.

'You mean — that it — it — ' She stammered and stopped.

'I mean,' he said in a low voice that was inaudible to Mirren and the vicar, 'that our appointment here for this morning is now rendered futile.'

'Surely,' she whispered, 'nobody would — would be so wicked. Why, Stiller might easily have been — have been — '

'I doubt if the person who did this would have cared very much if he had,' said the dramatist. 'He has already killed once, perhaps twice, and another death wouldn't worry him.'

'I hope you're wrong, Mr. Lowe,' said the girl. 'It's dreadful to think that there should be someone — like that — at large.'

'We can only hope that he won't be at

large for long,' said Lowe. 'He certainly won't if I can do anything to prevent it.'

She was silent, and he saw the fear in her eyes, and then it faded and she changed the subject abruptly.

'I had a rather extraordinary letter from Mr. Tempest's solicitor this morning,' she said. 'It appears that on going into his financial affairs there is a large sum of money missing which cannot be accounted for, and they want me to go up and see them. The appointment is for this morning, and I was going to ask you if you would come with me. There might be something in this missing money that would help, mightn't there?'

Lowe thought there certainly might. He remembered Mr. Hammerton's evidence at the inquest and the discrepancy between his estimate of Roger Tempest's fortune and the solicitor's.

The appointment was for eleven-thirty, and he suggested that he should call for the girl immediately after breakfast, a suggestion to which she agreed.

There was nothing more he could do at the ruins of the White House, and he returned to the Bull. It was nine-thirty when he called at the vicarage for the girl, and found her waiting for him at the end of the drive, and a man on a motorcycle who had followed him from the Bull, kept the big car in sight throughout its journey to London.

14

The Missing Money

Mr. Whittlesey's offices were in Bedford Row, and the lawyer was standing by his desk looking through a sheaf of papers when Lowe and the girl were shown in.

He greeted them pleasantly but rather pompously.

'Good morning, Miss Warren, good morning, Mr. Lowe,' he said. 'I am very glad you have come with this young lady, sir. She telephoned to say that she was bringing you, and I was more than pleased. Some curious points — some very curious points — have arisen which will have to be cleared up.'

He waved them into two shabby leather armchairs, and seated himself behind his desk. For a moment he consulted some documents in front of him, and then leaned forward.

'You will remember that at the inquest

the question of Mr. Tempest's estate was brought up by the Coroner?' he said.

Lowe nodded.

'Well,' went on Mr. Whittlesey, 'you will no doubt recall that whereas Mr. Hammerton, Mr. Tempest's literary agent, estimated the estate at one hundred and twenty thousand pounds, I was confident that the amount was nearer double that figure. Now, however, after checking up most carefully on the money available, I am astonished to find that Mr. Hammerton was more correct than I. Yet an inspection of the various contracts and royalty statements, which Mr. Hammerton, at my request has supplied me with, together with all the revenue from Mr. Tempest's investments, shows that I should be right in my estimate. There is exactly one hundred and thirty thousand pounds missing, money which should have been paid into Mr. Tempest's account by Mr. Hammerton.'

Lowe pursed his lips in a silent whistle. It was an enormous sum; certainly sufficient to provide a motive for a dozen murders.

'Have you asked Mr. Hammerton about this money?' he inquired; and the solicitor shook his head.

'No, not yet,' he replied. 'I wished to see if Miss Warren knew anything about it first. You see it was possible that Mr. Tempest might have used it for something, though what he could have done with a tremendous sum like that I am unable to conjecture. Do you know anything about it, Miss Warren?'

'No, Mr. Whittlesey,' she answered at once, 'I know nothing about it at all. You see, I had very little to do with Mr. Tempest's financial affairs, beyond attending to the household bills and various items like that. He used to say that I had plenty to do to keep pace with my own work, and that the money side of the business could safely be left to you and to Mr. Hammerton.'

'So far as I am concerned he was right,' said the lawyer, frowning. 'But with regard to Mr. Hammerton — ' His frown deepened. 'Well, really, I am not at all happy about Mr. Hammerton's position. All the money due to Mr. Tempest passed through his hands, and, well — ' He stopped and shook his head dubiously.

'You are suggesting that it would have been possible for Mr. Hammerton to have helped himself from time to time?' said Lowe and the solicitor admitted that he was.

'Are you aware that Mrs. Roger Tempest is acquainted with Hammerton?' continued the dramatist, and Mr. Whittlesey started.

'No, is she?' he asked. 'You know that was a great shock to me — a very great shock. I had no idea that Tempest was married until I received a letter from the — er — lady's solicitors informing me that she was contesting the will.'

'Oh, she's going to contest the will, is she?' remarked Lowe. 'I presume she has very little likelihood of being successful?'

'None whatever,' replied the lawyer. 'Although the marriage is quite legal — I have seen the certificate — I cannot understand why Tempest never told me that he was married.'

'That,' said the dramatist, 'is one of the things that I would like to know. Nobody, apparently, was aware that he was married. I realise, having seen the lady, that Mrs. Tempest was hardly the kind of person he would have wished to boast about, but why did he marry her at all? He must have known what she was like.'

'In my opinion,' answered Mr. Whittlesey, 'he got himself entangled with her, and was forced to marry her. That is the only explanation that I can offer. He certainly never lived with her. The marriage took place at the Brompton Road registrar's office, five years ago, and at that time Tempest was living at Long Dene. Isn't that right, Miss Warren?'

'Yes,' the girl nodded, 'and he never said a word about being married. I wasn't working for him then, but he was very friendly with both father and me. I'm sure he would have told us, unless there was some reason why he wanted to keep the matter a secret.'

'Well,' remarked Lowe, 'whatever the reason was he certainly succeeded in keeping his secret. Was Hammerton his agent at this time?'

'Yes,' said the lawyer, a little surprised at the question. 'He has always acted for Tempest. Why?'

'I was just wondering,' answered the dramatist evasively. 'I suppose you will be taking the matter of this missing money up with Hammerton?'

'Most certainly, now that I have seen Miss Warren and she has no knowledge of it,' replied Mr. Whittlesey.

'Then,' said Lowe, 'why not telephone him and ask him to come round now? I should very much like to hear what he has to say.'

The lawyer looked doubtful, but Lowe argued away his scruples.

'He is coming over at once,' he said, after a brief telephone conversation. 'I did not mention that you were here.'

While they awaited the arrival of the literary agent, Lowe asked Mr. Whittlesey several questions concerning Roger Tempest, but he learned no more than he already knew. So far as the lawyer was aware the dead man had not known Sir Horace Gladwin, or had any dealings with him. He was both startled and surprised when the dramatist, in reply to his question, explained his reason for asking, and he was still recovering from the shock when Mr. Hammerton was announced.

The literary agent came into the office confidently, though there was a heaviness about his eyes which told of worry and sleepless nights. At the sight of Lowe and Isabel, his confidence received something of a setback, apparently, for his expression changed, and his rather small eyes darted from one to the other suspiciously.

'This is an unexpected pleasure,' he said. 'I rather thought you would be alone, Whittlesey.'

'Miss Warren very kindly came to see if she could assist me in tracing certain monies of my late client's which appear to be missing,' said the lawyer, 'and Mr. Lowe, who is, as you know, investigating the matter of poor Tempest's death, very naturally came with her.'

'What is this money that's missing?' asked Hammerton.

'It is a large sum,' answered the lawyer; 'approximately one hundred and thirty thousand pounds, and there is no trace of it. It should have been paid into Tempest's bank with other amounts accruing from his contracts, but, so far as I can see, it has not been.'

'And for a very simple reason,' replied Mr. Hammerton easily. 'At Tempest's own request the money was paid to him in cash!'

The lawyer looked at him incredulously.

'Do I understand you to mean,' he said, 'that you paid this colossal sum to Mr. Tempest in cash instead of crediting his balance at the bank with this amount in the usual way?'

'Yes,' said Hammerton, nodding. 'Not in one sum, of course. That amount has been spread over a period, nearly four years I should say.'

'But this is most extraordinary,' exclaimed Mr. Whittlesey. 'Did Tempest say what he wanted this money for?'

'No,' replied the literary agent, 'and naturally I did not ask him. It was his own money, and he was entitled to have it in cash if he wished it. He gave receipts for the amounts as they were paid over to him, and that's all that concerned me.'

'Have you these receipts?' asked the lawyer quickly.

'You have them, haven't you?' said Hammerton, and when the other shook his head: 'I thought I sent them over to you with the rest of the documents.'

'I have seen nothing of them,' said Mr. Whittlesey. 'If I had I should not have wondered what had happened to this money.'

'No, of course not,' said the literary agent. 'I suppose I must have omitted to put them in with the rest. I'll send 'em over to you directly I get back to the office.'

He was perfectly cool and collected, and if what he had stated was true there was no reason why he should be anything else.

'I shall be very pleased if you will do so,' said the lawyer. 'I'm quite sure you didn't send them over with the other documents.'

'You shall have them first thing in the morning,' said the literary agent. He rose to his feet. 'If that is all you wish to see me about,' he went on a little stiffly, 'I should like to be getting back to my office.'

'There is nothing further at the moment,' said Mr. Whittlesey, and Hammerton took his leave.

When he had gone the lawyer looked across at Lowe.

'The question of the whereabouts of this money seems to me to be most important,' he said gravely.

'I agree with you,' answered the dramatist. 'It is most important, and may quite possibly have a bearing on Tempest's death.'

'It isn't as if it was a small sum,' said the lawyer, his thin fingers tapping nervously on the blotting pad in front of him. 'What could he have done with a hundred and thirty thousand pounds?'

'I can suggest several things,' answered Lowe, 'but I think what you have in mind is blackmail, Mr. Whittlesey, isn't it?'

The lawyer nodded reluctantly.

'It seems the most obvious conclusion to come to,' he answered. 'The fact that this amount never passed through his bank, but was paid to him, at his request, by Hammerton, in cash, seems to suggest to my mind no other alternative.'

'If it was ever paid to him!' said the dramatist quietly.

The lawyer jerked up his head with a startled expression.

'Are you suggesting that Hammerton is lying?' he inquired.

Lowe shook his head.

'No,' he said, 'I am not, but I am considering the possibility that he is. Let us suppose, for the sake of argument, that Hammerton has embezzled this money. This explanation of his would offer a very good cover, wouldn't it?'

'But the receipts?' protested Mr. Whittlesey. 'He says he has receipts for these various sums which he paid out to Tempest.'

'It would not be difficult,' said Lowe, 'to forge a receipt. Mind you, I'm not accusing Hammerton of anything. I'm merely suggesting a possible explanation for the disappearance of this money. There is no doubt that Hammerton and Mrs. Tempest are acquainted, how closely they are acquainted we do not know. It may be that she is mixed up in this matter — we don't know that either, but it's only by considering all these points that we're likely to find out the truth.'

He left the lawyer a few minutes later, a greatly worried and perplexed man, and when he and Isabel reached the car he turned to the girl.

'While I'm in town,' he said, 'I'm rather anxious to make a few further inquiries concerning Mr. Tempest. It will be rather tedious for you to remain with me, so can I drive you to some restaurant and pick you up later? I shall only be about an hour.'

She suggested Harridge's, and he dropped her at the big store in Oxford Street, arranging to meet her in the restaurant.

It was ten minutes over the stipulated time when he returned, for which he apologized, but though she looked at him inquiringly he said nothing concerning what he had learned during his absence.

As they drove back to Long Dene he was very thoughtful and silent, for his inquiries had provided him with a fact that, in view of what he had learned that afternoon, was of vital significance.

Mrs. Tempest lived in one of the largest of a block of flats overlooking Hyde Park. They were expensive flats; the rent of the one she occupied was six hundred and fifty pounds per annum. She lived in a style that was anything but cheap. She entertained lavishly, ran a staff of servants and kept a car and chauffeur as well as the sports model in which she had driven up to the Bull. He calculated that her minimal expenditure must be in the region of between two or three thousand a year, and, according to her solicitors, Roger Tempest's allowance had been a hundred pounds monthly. Where had the balance come from?

He was still pondering this question when he dropped Isabel at the vicarage and went back to the Bull.

15

The Eavesdropper

Inspector Mirren was talking to Arnold White in the vestibule when the dramatist arrived.

'I've been waiting for you, sir,' he said, 'and I was just going. The Chief Constable has decided to ask the help of the Yard over the Gladwin case. Sir Horace was a member of the County Council, as you know, and a pretty big bug generally, so I suppose they have more or less insisted on a London man being sent for to handle the affair.'

He was obviously disappointed, and Lowe did his best to soothe his injured feelings. It was only natural that Mirren should resent the interference of the Yard. This was a big case, and if he had been able to handle it on his own successfully, might have done him a lot of good.

'No news about Richard Tempest, I

suppose?' he asked, and Mirren shook his head.

'No,' he answered despondently, 'nothing at all. He's just vanished without any trace. I think that had a lot to do with the Chief Constable's attitude, though I don't see what more I could have done.'

'I'm sure you've done all you could, Inspector,' said Lowe. 'It's most extraordinary that Richard Tempest should have remained at large for so long.'

'It's a miracle,' declared Mirren. 'The whole country's searching for him — he must have made himself invisible. Well, perhaps the Yard people will have better luck. Did you discover anything in London, sir?'

'One or two fresh items,' said the dramatist, and told the Inspector of his discoveries concerning the missing money and Mrs. Tempest.

'It's certainly queer,' agreed Mirren, rubbing his chin, 'but the queerest thing to my mind is this fire. I don't see how that place could have caught fire if Stiller's telling the truth.'

'It caught fire,' said Lowe seriously,

after a pause, 'because someone deliber-ately set fire to it!'

The Inspector's eyes widened in astonishment.

'Deliberately set fire to it?' he echoed. 'What would anybody want to do that for?'

'I believe it was done,' said Lowe, 'for the purpose of destroying evidence.'

'What evidence?' demanded Mirren. 'We searched the place thoroughly. I am sure there was nothing we overlooked.'

'I'm referring,' said the dramatist, 'to the notes for a new story which Mr. Tempest had dictated to Miss Warren some time prior to his death.'

'The notes for a story?' said the bewildered Inspector. 'But why on earth should anyone want — ?'

'I'll tell you,' said Lowe, and repeated what the girl had told him on the previous evening.

When he had finished Mirren whistled softly.

'It does look rather odd, Mr. Lowe,' he said. 'You're suggesting, I suppose, that in some way the person who murdered Sir Horace had got hold of this plot of

Tempest's and used it for his own purpose?'

Lowe nodded.

'That seems the most plausible explanation,' he replied. 'Of course it's only a theory, but it's too much to believe that it's purely coincidence; though why poor Tempest should have been killed after being kept prisoner for eight days I don't know.'

'And you won't!' grunted Mirren, 'until we lay our hands on his brother, sir. I'll bet he's at the bottom of it, and the Gladwin business also. Well, sir, I must be on my way. I've got to go over to Minchester and see the Chief Constable. If anything further happens I'll let you know at once.'

He had only been gone ten minutes when the landlord of the Bull came into the vestibule to inform Lowe that he was wanted on the telephone.

The dramatist hurried across to the box, which stood on the far side near the entrance to the saloon bar. It was possible to see into the vestibule through the glass partition that separated it from the bar and a thin-faced man who had come in shortly after Lowe's arrival and was slowly sipping a whiskey and soda, saw him go into the telephone box, and moved closer to the wall. The back of the box actually formed part of the wall between the vestibule and the saloon bar, and it was possible to hear what was taking place for the partition was thin.

The dramatist stepped into the little cubicle, closed the door, and picking up the receiver held it to his ear.

The caller was Isabel and her voice was excited.

'Is that Mr. Lowe?' she said, and when he replied in the affirmative: 'I've found something which I think is rather important. You remember that furniture that was saved from the White House? Well, father told them to bring it over to the vicarage and we'd look after it. Mr. Tempest's desk was amongst it and I've found the notes of that plot I was telling you about.'

'Where did you find the notes, Miss Warren?' asked Lowe quickly.

'There was a large blotter in the middle

drawer,' answered the girl, 'and the notes were on three sheets of paper slipped in between the blotting paper. I have them here.'

'Keep them till I come,' said the dramatist. 'I will be with you in half an hour.'

He left the telephone box and returned to White, explaining hastily the gist of the call; but even before he had hung up the receiver the thin-faced man, who had been listening, slipped hurriedly out of the bar and went speeding away on the motorcycle which he had left leaning against the side of the inn for just such an emergency as this.

16

The Vanishing of Isabel

The man on the motorcycle did not go far. Halfway down the street stood a very new, and very glaringly painted telephone box.

Bringing his noisy machine to a stop he kicked down the stand and opening the glass door entered the cabinet. Spitting out the end of a cigar that he had been smoking, he lifted the receiver, dropped his coins into the slot, and huskily called a number. After the delay of a few seconds the voice he was waiting to hear came over the wire.

'This is Shorty, boss,' he said, hissing the words out of the side of his mouth in a manner that would have told its own story to any experienced police officer. 'We've got to move quick!'

'What is it?' asked the deep voice of the other sharply.

'That gal's found them notes, and that feller Lowe's on his way to get 'em!'

The other uttered a muffled oath, and there was a moment's silence. Then he started to speak rapidly, issuing a string of orders in low, quick tones.

The man who called himself Shorty listened, jerking his thin, narrow head now and again in a series of brief nods. Obviously the other knew Long Dene very well, for his instructions were explicit, and could only have been given by someone who was familiar with the village.

When he had finished, the thin-faced man snapped a hurried goodbye and rang off; but he didn't leave the box. Fumbling in his pocket he produced more coins and called another number. When the connection was made he spoke, and his voice had changed from the husky whisper to a rather stilted unnatural tone.

'Is that Miss Warren?' he said. 'This is the potman at the Bull speaking, Miss — '

★ ★ ★

160

The distance from the Bull Inn to the village was approximately half a mile, and Trevor Lowe decided that it was not worth getting out the car. Although he was anxious to secure the notes of Roger Tempest's story, which the girl had discovered, there was, so far as he knew, no intense hurry, so he set off with Arnold White at a leisurely pace towards the High Street.

There was hardly anyone about — they met two villagers either returning home or going to the Bull — and the only sound which broke the silence was made by a small saloon car which sped past them and disappeared round the bend. Neither of them gave it much attention, which was a pity, for both it and its driver were closely concerned with the events that were to come. There was nothing to tell them this, however, and so they strolled on, arriving presently at the vicarage.

In answer to the dramatist's ring the front door was opened by the little clergyman himself. When he saw who his visitors were his eyebrows lifted in an expression of astonishment.

'Why, Mr. Lowe,' he said, 'I didn't expect to see you!'

'I understood,' said Lowe, 'that Miss Warren expected us. Perhaps she didn't tell you that she phoned me a little while ago?'

The expression on the vicar's face became more surprised than ever.

'Of course I knew she phoned you!' he exclaimed, a note of anxiety creeping into his voice, 'but when your message came through asking her to meet you she hurried out at once. You must have missed her!'

Lowe's eyes narrowed.

'I sent her no message,' he said. 'She rang me up at the Bull about twenty minutes ago. She had found something of importance in the desk which was brought from the White House — '

'Yes — yes, I know that,' broke in the vicar, looking genuinely alarmed, 'but the potman at the Bull rang up and said he had been instructed by you to ask her to meet you at the police station. She was to take the notes she had found, there. I think, if I remember rightly, the man said there was some urgency as you might have to go to London at once. Naturally she hurried off immediately. Didn't you send that message?'

The dramatist shook his head.

'No,' he answered quickly, 'I didn't!'

'Then who could have — ?' began the agitated clergyman.

'Somebody who wanted to get hold of those notes,' interrupted Lowe. 'I don't like the sound of it at all!'

The vicar's face went pale.

'Do you mean — ' he gasped. 'Do you think that Isabel's in danger?'

The dramatist nodded, and his face had set grimly.

'I do!' he declared.

He got on to the supervisor at the telephone exchange.

'I'm speaking for the police,' he said briefly. 'A call was put through to the vicarage at Long Dene a quarter of an hour ago. I want to know from whence it emanated.'

While the supervisor endeavoured to discover, he waited, his fingers beating an impatient tattoo on the top of the little table. Presently the answer came through.

'There were two calls put through to the vicarage this evening,' said the voice of the supervisor. 'One was from Mr. Topwood, of South Avenue, and the other came from a call box in the High Street.'

'Do you know anyone called Topwood?' asked Lowe, when he had hurriedly thanked the supervisor and put down the receiver.

'Yes, yes,' said the vicar. 'Topwood is one of my churchwardens. What — ?'

But the dramatist was already halfway down the steps. Isabel Warren was in serious danger, and something had to be done quickly. She must be found — and found at once. The bogus message had definitely instructed her to go to the police-station, and since it had mentioned that the matter was urgent it was only reasonable to suppose that she would naturally take the nearest route. Whatever had happened to her had, therefore, happened between the vicarage and the quickest road to the police station. Explaining this hurriedly to White, the dramatist set off at a run, with his secretary at his heels.

The police station lay amid a cluster of small cottages on the other side of the Green, and the shortest cut was through a lane near the entrance to the vicarage drive. The girl must have gone this way: if she had gone any other they would have met her on the way down. She had probably turned into the lane just as they reached the garage on the corner of the High Street, but there was certainly no sign of her now.

They came out by the Post Office, and, out of the corner of his eye as he raced by, the dramatist saw the red telephone-box from which the unknown call had come. It might very well be worth looking at later, but there was no time to stop now.

They reached the Green and paused. With the exception of one or two dotted lights a black void stretched in front of them, with neither sound nor movement. Telling White to go in one direction, Lowe set off in the other to complete a circle of the Green. His eyes searched the blackness as he ran, and his ears were strained to catch the slightest sound that

165

might give him a clue to the whereabouts of the girl. As he passed the Long Dene War Memorial he thought he heard a faint cry, and stopped to listen; but it was not repeated, and he concluded that what he had heard had only been some night-bird in the trees which grew thickly a few yards away. He ran on and presently, beneath one of the few sparsely dotted lampposts, was joined by White. The secretary had met no one, neither had he heard any sound. They explored the Green, with no better result, and Lowe decided that to continue this aimless searching was only a useless waste of time. Isabel Warren had been spirited away, and she might quite easily be miles from that spot. There was only one thing to be done, and he did it without further delay. He made for the police station, discovering, when he got there, that Inspector Mirren had gone home. A direct line, however, connected his little cottage with the Station House, and in a few seconds the dramatist heard his voice at the other end of the wire, and quickly explained what had happened.

'All right, sir,' said Mirren, 'I'll come over. We'll have a description circulated at once. By the way I've received notification from Scotland Yard that Detective-Inspector Shadgold is on his way down.'

'I'm glad of that,' said Lowe. 'I know him very well. We've worked together many times before. When is he arriving?'

'The train reaches Minchester at 10.10,' replied Mirren. 'I'm having a car to meet him. He'll probably like to put up at the Bull with you.'

'I should like to see him as soon as he gets here,' said Lowe, and hung up the receiver. He could safely leave the routine enquiries to the Inspector, and he was anxious to have a look at the public telephone-box from which the bogus call to the vicarage had emanated. With a word to the sergeant in charge he left the little station house and strode across the Green in the direction of the High Street.

Obviously the girl had been taken because of those notes that she had found. That was the motive behind whatever had happened to her, and that meant that someone must have discovered that they were in her possession. Since she had telephoned to the Bull practically immediately after she had made the discovery, the person who had planned the abduction — or whatever it was — must have overheard that message, either at the vicarage end, or at the Bull. The question that worried him most was whether the girl herself was in any danger. If the person or persons to whom these notes were of value only wanted to obtain possession of them, then there was no reason why she should be. On the other hand, the unknown had already killed twice — if it was permissible to conclude that the same person who had killed Roger Tempest had also been responsible for the murder of Sir Horace Gladwin — and was not likely to hesitate to kill again if it suited his purpose. The result of Isabel Warren's disappearance had, however, definitely proved one thing. A vigilant watch was being kept on his — Lowe's — movements.

He reached the telephone-box. Perhaps there would be a clue here that would tell him the identity of the watcher.

17

The Clue in the 'Phone Box

When the thin-faced man left the telephone-box in the High Street, his lips were curled back in an unpleasant grin. It was a clever scheme that his employer had hastily explained — clever because it must have been thought out on the spur of the moment. This wizened-faced little crook had a perverted sense of humour, and it appealed to him.

Getting astride his motorcycle he set off at full speed towards the Green pulling up at last near the Long Dene War Memorial. The old tank loomed out of the darkness like some prehistoric monster, a mass of half-rusted metal, patched greyly where the paint remained, and bearing little semblance to the once formidable instrument of war which had ploughed victoriously through the mud of Flanders.

The man called Shorty glanced about

him, and, assured that he was unobserved propped his bicycle against a nearby tree and went over to the small steel door that lay behind the projecting gun turret. It was shut and locked, but this man had done time for opening doors that were shut and locked and producing a little leather roll from his pocket he set to work, keeping a vigilant eye open for the slightest sign of a possible interruption. In a few seconds the rusted lock clicked back, and the door opened to the accompaniment of a protesting squeak. With a breath of relief he closed it again, leaving it unlocked. Once more he went back to his cycle, started the engine and turned into the lane that formed a short cut to the vicarage gate. Halfway along this he stopped, pulled his machine into the shelter of a clump of bushes, and waited. He was ready now for the next part of the programme. In a few seconds he heard a light, hurried step approaching, and peering out from the concealment of the bushes, saw faintly in the gloomy dusk of the lane, the figure of the girl as she hurried towards him. He had timed it nicely. With lips slightly parted he crouched — tense. On she came, walking quickly, and as she drew level with him he sprang forward. She had no time to utter more than a startled cry, stifled instantly by the hand that came quickly up over her mouth. He held her helpless while the lean fingers of his other hand sought her throat. She struggled frantically, but in spite of his smallness, Shorty was strong. The fingers pressed cruelly into the soft flesh of her neck, and presently her struggles ceased and she hung limp in his arms. He laid her down and looked at her anxiously. This was not to be a killing, and he was reassured when, under his hand, he felt her heart still beating.

A quick glance round and he saw the handbag that she had been carrying. Opening it, he hastily extracted a folded envelope, thrust it into his pocket, and still retaining the bag, picked the girl up and carried her over to the motorcycle. Resting her across the saddle, he pushed the machine as fast as he could back to the Green. The oblong strip of grass was still deserted, and laying the girl down in the shadow of the old tank he hurriedly bound her wrists and ankles with some cord that he took from his pocket. Not satisfied with this, he fashioned an improvised gag from one of her stockings and a handkerchief and securely knotted it round her mouth.

Isabel recovered consciousness just as he finished, and began to struggle. But the cords had been tied tightly and she was helpless.

The thin-faced man picked her up and carried her inside the tank, and after a second came out — alone. Closing and locking the door, he gave a hasty glance round to assure himself that he had not been seen, and, mounting his cycle, went roaring away into the darkness.

★　★　★

Trevor Lowe stood for a moment outside the public call box at the corner of the High Street and looked about him. It was unlikely that in a small village like Long Dene the box would be used very frequently, less likely that another call

172

would have been put through that night, after the one which had been received by Isabel Warren at the vicarage. Therefore it was possible that some trace of the unknown caller might be found.

He opened the door of the little kiosk and slipped inside. The first thing of which he became aware was the rank smell of stale cigar smoke. There was ash on the little wooden desk near the mouthpiece of the telephone, and a further examination brought to light the trodden-on butt of a cigar. He picked it up and looked at it. The end had been badly chewed, and it appeared to be of a rather cheap brand. There was no certainty that it had belonged to the person who had put through the bogus call, but there was at least a possibility, and he put it away carefully in an envelope which he found in his pocket. Later it might prove of value. What interested him most just then was the fact that, if the last person to use the telephone had been concerned in the disappearance of the girl, then there was a distinct probability that that person had left fingerprints on the vulcanite of the instrument — always supposing, of course, that he had not taken the precaution of wearing gloves.

He had nothing with which to test this possibility, but it was essential that the cabinet should not be used until after such a test had been made.

He searched in his pockets, produced a pencil, and, tearing a sheet from his notebook, he wrote in capital letters: OUT OF ORDER. This notice he stuck with two pieces of stamp-paper against the glass on the inside of the door. As a further precaution, he succeeded in wedging the door fairly firmly with a box of matches. When he had done this he returned to the Police Station.

There was a car outside and the reason for its presence was revealed when he entered the little charge-room. A big, thick-set, burly man was standing by the small fireplace.

'Hello, Shadgold,' greeted the dramatist, 'I am glad to see you. Have you got your 'murder bag' with you?'

Detective-Inspector Shadgold nodded.

'Yes, it's in the car, Mr. Lowe,' he replied. 'Why?'

Lowe explained quickly.

'Good idea!' said Shadgold approvingly. 'Though, of course if this person hasn't been through our hands the prints won't tell us much.'

'It's worth trying, anyway,' replied the dramatist, and they set off.

When they reached the box, Shadgold unpacked the 'murder bag' which is carried by every Scotland Yard officer engaged on a murder case, and contains a selection of such things as may be useful in the investigation, and set to work.

'Plenty of prints here, all right,' he grunted. 'Dozens of 'em!'

He took several flashlight photographs of the telephone, after he had brought up the prints with the aid of a white powder sprayed over the instrument.

'I'll get these rushed to the Yard tonight,' he said when he had finished, 'and we ought to have any information there is, by breakfast time tomorrow.'

There was nothing else to be done at the moment, and Lowe suggested that they should go back to the Bull for a drink. Shadgold agreed with alacrity, and after stopping at the Police Station to dispatch a messenger to Scotland Yard with the photographs of the prints, they made their way to the inn.

Lowe expected to find Arnold White there, but there was no sign of him. He concluded that the secretary was probably still having a look round, and ordering drinks for himself and the Inspector, settled down in the lounge to tell Shadgold all he knew about the business which had brought him to Long Dene. And while they talked Arnold White lay unconscious on the Green, his white face upturned to the lowering sky.

18

What Happened to White

There was no real reason why Arnold White should have elected to go back to the Bull by way of the Green except that it occurred to him to have a final look round for some trace of the girl.

The oblong strip of grass was empty, a wide expanse unbroken except for the grotesque shape of the old tank propped up on its concrete base.

He was passing with only a glance at the relic, when he thought he saw something move in its shadow, and stopping he made out the vague figure of a man. As silently as he could, Arnold crept nearer. It might be only one of the villagers waiting to keep an appointment, but on the other hand it might not.

Apparently it was not, for as he drew near to the old memorial, the man made off and disappeared in the shadow of a clump of trees.

'Queer!' muttered the secretary to himself, as he stood by the mass of rusted metal and looked about him. 'What was he up to, I wonder.'

And then he almost jumped out of his skin as there came a succession of dull thuds at his elbow. They sounded as though somebody was banging on the other side of the old tank, and he ran round to see who it was, but there was nobody there!

The thudding, however, continued and he was forced to the conclusion that it came from inside! It seemed impossible, and to make sure he pressed his ear to the metal door. The thudding did come from inside the tank. And that was all he remembered for some time. At that moment the sky fell with the weight of many tons, and all sound and sight was blotted out by the rush of painful darkness that flooded his brain . . .

Trevor Lowe glanced at the clock and frowned.

'I wonder where White's got to?' he

muttered. 'He ought to have got back here by now.'

'Dropped in for a drink somewhere, perhaps,' suggested Shadgold.

The dramatist shook his head.

'There isn't another pub about here,' he answered. 'I think, if you don't mind, Shadgold, I'll go and see if I can see anything of him.'

'I'll come with you,' replied the Inspector.

The police car was outside, and Shadgold took the wheel. They drove slowly along the deserted High Street, passed the scarlet callbox, and presently came out by the side of the Green. But they saw no sign of White.

It was Trevor Lowe who first saw the wide-open door of the army tank as Shadgold swung past in the car.

'Stop, Shadgold!' The dramatist's tone was authoritative, and the C.I.D. man immediately braked the car to a standstill. 'What the . . . ' He stopped with a gasp, for in the steady beam of the car's headlights it was not difficult for him to recognise the inanimate, sprawling figure of White who lay in front of them. He was out of the car and racing to the spot in a flash. Behind him, labouring under his greater weight, came Detective-Inspector Shadgold. Kneeling beside the still figure of his secretary he made a swift examination and exclaimed his relief aloud.

'Knocked out . . . thank God it's nothing worse!' He glanced up, puzzled by the open door of the tank. 'Have a look inside that tank will you, Shadgold?'

The detective switched on his electric torch and disappeared from view. When he returned he carried the torn remains of a woman's stocking and a folded handkerchief.

'H'm!' grunted Lowe. 'Is that all?'

'What did you expect me to find? Next year's Derby winner?' growled Shadgold; and the dramatist made no reply.

He turned his attention to reviving his secretary. In five minutes the young man came round, but he could tell them little. He spoke of a mysterious, ghost-like thudding from within the tank and then that sudden blow from behind. Who his assailant was he hadn't the foggiest idea.

'Tough luck,' sympathised Lowe.

'Tough skull, you mean,' chuckled Shadgold. 'But what's it all mean. anyway?'

'It means that we shall find one of our trails cleared up,' replied the dramatist. 'You can take it from me that Miss Warren is no longer missing, She'll be back at the vicarage by the time we get there. Come on.'

Between them they assisted White to the car. In the cold, revivifying night air he made a swift recovery.

Trevor Lowe's lips were set grimly when the car pulled up at the vicarage and the Vicar himself came forward to meet them.

'Mr. Lowe . . . my daughter . . . my daughter is all right. She's in her room now.'

'Is that so?' smiled Lowe with a queer expression. 'Do you think she will see me?'

'I can't make sense of what she tells me,' said the Vicar. 'Perhaps, Mr. Lowe, you'll be able to sort it all out.'

It was a strange story Isabel had to tell.

She described how she had been attacked . . . how she had been rendered unconscious . . . how, when she came to, her bag was gone . . . also her assailant.

'And where were you, Miss Isabel . . . when you came to?' asked the dramatist, his all-seeing eyes swift to notice the red, angry weals round her wrists.

'In the woods.' Isabel's tone lacked conviction. She crimsoned under the stare Lowe gave her. 'I — I — just wandered back here. Can't . . . can't remember any more.'

Trevor Lowe nodded politely. Unlike the others, he had observed that the girl was wearing only one stocking. She was keeping something back, that was obvious. When Shadgold, White and the Vicar wandered off for refreshment Lowe took the girl gently by the arm.

'Supposing, Miss Warren, now that we are alone, you tell me exactly what did happen?' he suggested.

She tore herself away from him, her pretty face alive with alarm and apprehension.

'Mr. Lowe . . . I — I've told you

everything!' She returned him look for look. Without the quiver of an eyelid. 'Everything . . . '

'Then there is nothing more to be said, of course,' said Lowe genially. 'I beg your pardon.'

His manner was quite disarming, and Isabel Warren showed her relief in a broad smile. She would not, however, have been so relieved could she have read the other's thoughts . . . He knew that she was not telling the truth. She had been imprisoned in the tank. Someone had rescued her, someone whose identity she wanted to hide.

19

Shorty Gets His Reward

'Hand over the notes!' Shorty's boss was impatient and his voice carried a grim note. 'What the devil are you grinning at?'

Shorty continued to grin . . . a crafty, leering grin that stirred the impatient man into a fresh tirade of abuse.

'You little rat! If you don't stop grinning like a Cheshire cat and hand over the stuff I'll — I'll — '

'You'll what?' jeered Shorty. 'You'll do nothing, see? This time, Mr. Clever-dick it's me that's doing the talking. Me that's giving the orders, see? Put that in your pipe and smoke it. I've got the papers all right — '

'And the girl? You put her — her body where I suggested?' The other changed his tone to a somewhat more conciliatory one.

Shorty winked expressively at the ceiling.

'I got the girl all right, and I put her where you said. And I've got the stuff she carried, but before you handle it you'll give me a thousand quid in exchange for it. Do I make myself clear?'

The other whistled his dismay. He had underestimated Shorty. This man had more spirit, more intelligence than he had bargained for.

'Do you know what you're asking? A thousand pounds! Haven't I paid you a tenner already?'

Shorty sniffed. 'A tenner! What's the good of a tenner to me? I've got something you want, haven't I? Something that'll save your neck from the rope, too! And you think you can get it from me for a tenner. Well, you think again!'

Coolly he helped himself to a choice cigar from the box on the table. With the same coolness he helped himself to a very liberal drink of whiskey and soda. Shorty knew he had the whip hand, and, like many a rogue before him, the knowledge of his power made him greedy.

If the other man had underestimated Shorty, so now Shorty made the same mistake. All he could read in the heavy features before him was fear. A little more intelligence on Shorty's part and he would have seen a grim, sinister purpose behind the man's apparently apprehensive expression.

'Come, Shorty! You and I are old friends. We don't want to quarrel, do we?'

'Not me!' exclaimed Shorty, lighting up his cigar and puffing it like a man who smokes cigars only on Christmas Day and other occasions of national celebration. 'But we'll be better friends, Boss, when you hand me the thousand quid!'

'All right!' The other's heavy face broke into a cordial smile which completely deceived Shorty. 'I haven't the money on me now, naturally. Come round tomorrow, in the afternoon, and I'll give you the money. You'll take great care of those notes, won't you?'

Shorty puffed himself up with pride. He tapped his breast pocket and winked significantly.

'Trust me, Boss. Tomorrow then.' He grabbed some cigars, poured himself out another stiff whiskey and drained it at a gulp before he took his farewell.

The man he left forced a smile that he was far from feeling. Somehow he'd got to get the precious notes off Shorty without paying that fabulous price of a thousand pounds for them.

Whether it was the whiskey Shorty had consumed, or the jubilation of his greedy little heart, but his course along the main road Londonwards was erratic to a degree. Motorists, passing him, yelled their censure, but Shorty replied in a language that would burn any paper on which it was printed.

He was going to be rich . . . very rich. Once the Boss had paid a thousand quid for the notes, which were safely tucked in his jacket pocket, he was going to be made to realise that the thousand was merely a first instalment. It was too easy, thought Shorty, as he sped along on his motorbike; he wouldn't have to work again for a living!

He liked this train of thought, and turned it round in his mind as he tore along the highway. Then retribution overtook him in the shape of a saloon car which was speeding at sixty miles an hour to Shorty's thirty.

The nearside wing of the big saloon hit the wobbling motorbike with a tremendous crash, lifting it clear of the highway and throwing the bewildered Shorty about two dozen yards in the air before, with bone-crunching force, he hit the highway again head foremost.

From the driver of the saloon came a wild yell. He slammed on his brakes and brought the car to a stop within a foot of where Shorty lay sprawled in the road, a dark, ominous pool of crimson already staining the tarmac.

It was the first time Mr. Sheldon had ever met with a car accident, and his red, plump face was full of horror as he leapt from the driving seat and rushed across to that still, silent figure. He was stooping over Shorty's crumpled body when a patrol car drew alongside. Two uniformed officers stepped out.

'What's happened here . . . ? Accident?' asked the senior officer, rather unnecessarily.

Mr. Sheldon's plump face was set in a

mould of tragedy as he turned to explain.

'The man was zig-zagging all over the road. It wasn't my fault, Officer. He must have been drunk or something. It's terrible — terrible. But it wasn't my fault!'

'H'm!' grunted the officer. 'That's your story. Looks to me as if this fellow's badly damaged . . . '

'I've — I've not killed him?' gasped Mr. Sheldon. 'Do you mean that — that he won't live?'

'From what I can see it looks very much like it,' was the reply, and turning to his assistant: 'Radio to the nearest hospital for an ambulance.'

Agitated, and turning hot and cold by turns, Mr. Sheldon hovered on the tragic spot until the ambulance arrived. All this time Shorty had remained still and unconscious.

With great care the ambulance men lifted the body of his victim into the van, and the stolid expression on their faces seemed to tell Mr. Sheldon that there was not much hope for Shorty.

Mr. Sheldon was beside himself with anxiety.

'Poor fellow . . . it's terrible. It wasn't my fault. Can I come along to the hospital? I — I —'

'The best thing you can do, sir,' said the officer, a little touched by Mr. Sheldon's distress, 'is to come along to the station and make a statement about this and then go home.'

But Mr. Sheldon could not bring himself to do that. After leaving the station he went along to the hospital and hung around the waiting room, pumping nurses and attendants with weary monotony.

'No, the gentleman hasn't regained consciousness. The doctor doesn't expect him to . . . Compound fracture of the skull. That poor devil's as good as buried,' and so on.

It was the nurse who was bringing Shorty's clothes from the ward to place them in one of the lockers who seemed to quieten Mr. Sheldon more than anyone else had been able to do.

'Really, Mr. Sheldon, you mustn't worry yourself like this. Why don't you go home? There's no sense in hanging around here.' She smiled kindly at him as she went through the injured man's pockets in search of some means of identifying him. 'H'm! He doesn't seem to have anything on him that will help us to notify his people.'

She replaced the few possessions Shorty had carried on his person, folded the clothes, and then placed them in a locker numbered 437.

With a miserable face Mr. Sheldon watched her close the locker, and then, with a deep sigh of hopelessness, he turned on his heel and slowly went out of the hospital. The sound of his car starting up told the nurse that her advice was being carried out. She smiled tolerantly and settled down to while away the time before she should be relieved.

$$\star \quad \star \quad \star$$

It was an hour before dawn when a dark, shadowy figure entered the small hospital and tiptoed up to the reception counter. The nurse was dozing. Her eyes opened wide as some instinct warned her of danger, and her lips parted to yell, but nothing save a gurgle escaped her throat, and that choked away into silence as strong, vicious fingers closed round her windpipe and throttled her into unconsciousness.

The intruder, unrecognisable in the wide-brimmed felt hat which was pulled down low over his forehead and the upturned collar of a dark blue overcoat, acted with swiftness the moment the nurse collapsed.

The door of locker 437 was swung open in a flash. Shorty's jacket was snatched from the pile and a questing hand dived into the inside pocket, withdrawing a folded wad of papers. Hurriedly, the jacket was tossed back into the locker and the door closed. And as silently and as swiftly as he had come the mystery man departed.

20

The Clue of the Fingerprint

Trevor Lowe's manner was eager as he entered the dining room of the Bull five minutes after Detective-Inspector Shadgold and Arnold White had sat down at the breakfast table.

'Anything arrived — apart from this?' said the dramatist, pointing to a large dish of eggs and bacon, which graced the centre of the table.

The C.I.D. man chuckled.

'You're lucky, Mr. Lowe. Guess whose prints were found on that telephone receiver?' And as he spoke he opened a stout-looking envelope, which had arrived by the first train.

'Haven't the foggiest idea, Shadgold.'

'Shorty Fabin!' exclaimed the Inspector. 'Remember him? Thin-faced wisp of a man with a passion for picking locks.'

Lowe whistled as he screwed up his

193

brows in recollection.

'I remember him. He went down for a stretch four years ago, didn't he? Didn't know he was due out yet.'

'He wouldn't have been but for some trouble at the prison,' replied Shadgold. 'Shorty Fabin went to the assistance of a warder who was being attacked, and by doing that earned himself a handsome remission. They let him loose six months ago. Here, have a look at his picture. That will bring him back to your mind.'

The dramatist smiled grimly as he looked at the set of photographs Scotland Yard had sent. He remembered Shorty Fabin now, though his connection with this case was a mystery.

'He's the feller who phoned from that box, anyway,' went on Shadgold. 'The other prints checked up with respectable folks, leastways we have no record of them. What do you make of it, Mr. Lowe? And what are you going to do?'

'I'm going to make short work of three rashers of that excellent-looking bacon and two eggs,' replied Trevor Lowe with a smile. 'And providing you two gluttons leave enough toast and marmalade — '

And until he had made good his statement he refused to think that his day's work had started. Whatever programme he had planned received a setback when the local Inspector came into the Bull.

'Hello, Mirren!' exclaimed the dramatist cheerfully. 'Why this honour so early?'

But there was no mirth in Inspector Mirren's face when he replied.

'The one person we all would like to ask a few questions has done the dirty on us!' he announced gloomily.

'Eh?' Lowe, Shadgold and Arnold White voiced the exclamation together.

Inspector Mirren nodded emphatically.

'Soon as Inspector Shadgold put me wise to this Shorty Fabin I spread my net,' he explained. 'I didn't have to spread it far. It appears that Shorty Fabin was lying in Bell-Vue Hospital with a fractured skull — '

Lowe forgot the rest of his breakfast in this new turn of affairs.

'What happened to him, Mirren?'

'Patrol men report, after checking up

with other motorists on the route, that this feller Shorty Fabin was riding a motorbike towards London late last night and swerving all over the place.'

'Drunk — ' put in Shadgold.

'Seems like it,' said Mirren. 'Apparently more than one motorist complained of his erratic driving, and reported him. But it was left to a local man to run him over — and — and he's dead!'

'Killed him?' jerked Lowe with a frown.

'Sure! Mr. Sheldon did it — you know, the fat, jovial, old chap. The architect — '

'H'm!' said Trevor Lowe thoughtfully. 'How did it happen?'

'Usual stuff,' Mirren smiled sourly. 'Shorty Fabin was helping himself to both sides of the road when Mr. Sheldon came along in his saloon. Sheldon's nearside wing caught Shorty, and Shorty went to hospital in the ambulance.'

'And now he's dead,' said the dramatist. 'Just our luck.'

'Dead as anyone can be,' declared Inspector Mirren without enthusiasm. 'Never regained consciousness. But that isn't all.'

'Isn't that enough?' growled Shadgold. 'What is it?'

'During the night the nurse in the reception hall at the hospital was choked into unconsciousness by an unknown man. She couldn't describe him, except that he wore a wide-brimmed hat and kept his coat collar turned up.'

'Go on, man. Go on!' protested Shadgold, as Mirren paused to take a very necessary breath.

'The motive for the assault is clear enough,' went on Mirren. 'An inspection of the Shorty Fabin's effects shows that a wad of papers have disappeared. You can guess what those papers are, Mr. Lowe.'

'The notes of the plot which Roger Tempest drew up just before his death,' said Lowe slowly. 'They must be very incriminating for the master mind behind this entanglement to go to all the trouble he has. First Isabel Warren is kidnapped, then an innocent nurse is attacked, all to get hold of these precious papers.' He shook his head. 'We are getting into deep water,' he said dryly, 'and there are no clues?'

Inspector Mirren shook his head.

'I've just come from the hospital. Nothing to be found there — except that snivelling fool who keeps telling everyone that it wasn't his fault Shorty Fabin died.'

'You mean Mr. Sheldon?' asked Trevor Lowe. 'He seems to have taken it badly.'

'He certainly has!' said the Inspector. 'He was crying like a baby when I left.'

'He's very early at the hospital — ' began the dramatist, but Mirren smiled and interrupted.

'It's the old story. It wasn't his fault and he couldn't sleep. Sheldon apparently arrived at the hospital just after dawn, worrying the nurses for news of the man he had collided with. Personally I thought his tears were a bit overdone. Still, I suppose every man gets a weak moment now and again.'

'Yes,' said Lowe, and the tone in which he voiced that single word suggested that his thoughts were miles away from the subject under discussion.

'So all your fingerprint clue amounts to Mr. Lowe, is a dead man. This is some tangle!'

Trevor Lowe's lips set grimly.

'Well, it's checkmate for the moment, but I'll see this case through if I have to work on it for the next five years! There's only one thing that stands out to me at this early stage' — and here he looked fixedly at Inspector Mirren — 'and that is that Richard Tempest is as guiltless of his brother's killing as you are, Mirren!'

'Are you still certain of that, Mr. Lowe?' asked Inspector Mirren, with an uneasy smile.

'As certain as night follows day!' said Lowe with warmth. He rose to his feet and signalled to his secretary. 'Come on, White, let's get some exercise before we settle down to work. I'll see you later, Shadgold,' he said and with his secretary left the room.

'I wonder what's on his mind,' said Shadgold, when Lowe had gone.

'Don't ask me,' said Mirren. 'I'm used to working on official lines, sir, same as you. This Mr. Lowe is too unorthodox for me. He's got some bee in his bonnet.'

And in that sagacious remark Inspector Mirren wasn't far from the truth.

Back at the Bull Lowe discovered that Mr. Whittlesey, the lawyer, had been trying to get him on the telephone.

'He's found out something,' smiled Lowe to his secretary, as he picked up the instrument and asked for the lawyer's phone number. 'Perhaps we are getting somewhere.'

The expression on his employer's face told the secretary that this was not the case as he listened to the conversation.

'You say Hammerton has sent round the receipts, Mr. Whittlesey, and that they are all in order . . . ? The missing hundred and thirty thousand is now properly accounted for?' said Lowe, and there was disappointment in his voice.

'Every penny is now accounted for,' came the voice of the lawyer over the wire. 'The receipts date back over a period of four years. Each one is properly signed, stamped and dated with the indisputable signature of my late client, Mr. Roger Tempest. I thought, Mr. Lowe, you would be interested to receive confirmation of Mr. Hammerton's statement made in your hearing. That is why I telephoned you.'

Trevor Lowe was about to replace the receiver when a thought seemed to strike him.

'I should hate to appear overbearing, Mr. Whittlesey,' he said, 'but would you do me the favour of keeping those receipts handy until I can get to Town? In other words, don't file them away in your vault until I've had the opportunity of seeing them.'

'Certainly, Mr. Lowe,' came the reply. 'When can I expect you?'

'By lunch time,' replied the dramatist, and hung up.

'Get the car out,' he said briskly to his secretary. 'We're going to Town. Mr. Whittlesey declares that the receipts Hammerton sent him are in order. Maybe they are, but I'm going to satisfy myself on that point. You don't often hear me say I've got a hunch, but I've got one now, and against all my usual inclinations I'm going to follow it.'

He was impatient to be off, and Shadgold and Mirren, observing him pacing in the vestibule, felt constrained to ask him what it was all about.

'I've got an idea, and if it turns out wrong you can call me a prize idiot.' He said no more, for at that moment White drove up with the car, and with a smile at the C.I.D. man and the local Inspector he hurried away.

'He's not telling us too much,' said Mirren with a frown. 'I wonder what this idea is?'

'I expect it's that bee in his bonnet you referred to before,' growled Shadgold. 'I'm going to have a glass of something stronger than tea. Coming?'

Inspector Mirren accepted the invitation with a cough and a sly wink.

While the two Inspectors broke the rules of the force they both served, Trevor Lowe and White were speeding towards London with the accelerator pedal down on the floorboards for the best part of the journey.

Mr. Whittlesey was astonished to see them so soon, and said as much.

'You must have broken more than one speed limit on your journey from Long Dene,' he chided.

'You must blame my secretary,' said the

dramatist. 'I always leave him to drive when I want to think and I never bother to look at the speedometer. Now, Mr. Whittlesey, I should like to see those receipts that Mr. Hammerton has sent you.'

A few moments later the dramatist was closely examining the rather dog-eared pile of receipts the lawyer handed to him. They dated back, as he had said, over a period of four years, and each bore a twopenny stamp, across which sprawled the signature of Roger Tempest.

'You think the signatures might be forgeries, Mr. Lowe?'

'That was in my mind, Mr. Whittlesey,' answered Lowe, and there was an expression of disappointment on his face as he handed them back to the elder man. 'I can see nothing wrong with them, and I've made a close study of Mr. Tempest's signature.'

'Take it from me, Mr. Lowe,' said the lawyer, 'that those signatures are genuine.'

'It would appear I've had my journey for nothing,' said Lowe with a tired smile.

He said goodbye to the lawyer, and Mr.

Whittlesey accompanied them to the door. There was a knowledgeable smile on his wrinkled face as he gazed after the car.

'These amateurs always think they know better than the old hands,' he remarked to himself. 'Still, Trevor Lowe is a likeable fellow — shouldn't like him to be on my trail.'

He turned back into his stuffy office, carefully stacked the receipts together and bound them securely with a number of rubber bands. Then he dismissed the matter of Mr. Hammerton and the missing one hundred and thirty thousand pounds from his mind.

'Any luck, sir?' Arnold White ventured the question as his employer sat beside him with a strange glow of triumph on his face.

'The best. The very best,' said the dramatist. 'Drive to Hammerton's office. I think I've got that man where I want him.'

'I gather that the receipts Mr. Whittlesey seems so satisfied with are forgeries?'

'And very clever ones, too,' was the

reply. 'I can understand the signature deceiving Mr. Whittlesey, but Mr. Hammerton made one blunder.'

The secretary was aching to know what the blunder was, but not until the car had travelled for nearly a mile did Lowe continue his explanation, and then just as if there had been no stop in the conversation.

'Who sat on the throne of England four years ago, White?' he asked with a smile.

'On the throne?' asked White wonderingly. 'Why, King George of course. George the Fifth!'

'Then Mr. Hammerton will have to explain how it is that his early receipts, ostensibly made out when George the Fifth was King, bear stamps with the head of our present king — George the Sixth!'

In his astonishment White nearly let go of the driving wheel.

'Is that where he tripped up?' he asked.

'He most certainly did,' chuckled the dramatist. 'And that is what I want to see him about. Perhaps he'll talk when I tackle him with that.'

'And old Whittlesey didn't spot it,'

laughed White. 'He's a downy old bird, too.'

'And he's not the first downy old bird to be caught by a crook with a flair for forgery. Here we are,' he said, as the car glided up to the offices of Mr. Hammerton. 'Wait here, I don't suppose I shall be long.'

His face was grim as he got from the car, and neither he nor his secretary caught a glimpse of the terrified man who, from behind the cover of the curtain, observed his arrival.

21

Mr. Hammerton Panics

'Greville! Greville, you deaf old fool! Here, quickly!'

Mr. Hammerton's face was an unhealthy shade of grey as he peered round the door of his office and beckoned to his chief clerk.

Greville went over to his agitated employer.

'What is it, sir?' he asked, peering over the top of his metal-rimmed spectacles.

'Greville, I'm not in,' he said in an agitated voice. 'I'm not in, you understand. I'm not in to anybody! There's someone calling to see me and I don't want to see him. Tell him that I've had to go out of town — that I shan't be back until tomorrow.'

'Very good, sir,' said Greville, and he shrugged his bewilderment at the obvious agitation in his employer's face and manner. He was still more bewildered when the caller gave his name as Trevor Lowe. Some chord of memory connected the name of Lowe with crime and criminals in the ageing brain of Greville.

'I'm sorry, sir, but Mr. Hammerton is out of town. Called away, sir, you know. Urgently. Won't be back, I'm afraid, until — until tomorrow.'

The clerk did his task well. Not a muscle of his face betrayed him as he lied so glibly, and for the moment Lowe was deceived.

It was only when he caught sight of the expressions of the rest of the staff, reflected in a mirror that he was facing, that he knew Greville was lying.

'You must be wrong,' he said with a disarming smile. 'Mr. Hammerton arranged an appointment with me for this morning. I'll wait for him in his office, if you don't mind.'

And the latter phrase was couched in such a way as to indicate, whether Greville liked it or not, the dramatist was going into that inner office to wait for Hammerton.

'But — but — ' said Greville, and then gave it up with a gulp of resignation, for Lowe had pushed gently past him and was already opening the door marked 'Private'.

Had he been a second earlier in his arrival he would have seen a very startled literary agent darting for cover, As it was there was no sign of Mr. Hammerton when the dramatist strode in, though a still smouldering cigarette told its own tale . . .

Lowe smiled grimly as he observed it. He was convinced that the man he wanted to see was still in the room. Deliberately he sat down at Hammerton's desk and eyed the two large screens, which stood one at each end of the office. The dramatist knew that the agent must be behind one of them, for there was no other way of leaving that room than by the door through which he had entered.

'Come out, Hammerton,' he said. 'You can't fool me. I know you are here and I'll wait until you show yourself if I sit here all day! Come out!' His voice was authoritative, and his face hardened as he watched alternately the two screens.

Mr. Hammerton obliged with a suddenness that surprised the dramatist. The cupboard immediately behind the chair in which Lowe was sitting swung open suddenly. There, wild-eyed and desperate, stood the agent, a thick, ebony ruler in his hand.

Even as Trevor Lowe swivelled in the chair, when the first sound of the swinging door reached him, the ebony ruler flashed down with sickening force.

The dramatist collapsed without a moan. Over him stood Hammerton, ruler upraised as if to strike again. And then it seemed as if he had control of himself, and for a moment stood still, thinking rapidly. Stunning a man with a ruler was one thing but killing him with it was vastly different, and might result in the unpleasant feeling of a rope around his neck, and Mr. Hammerton had no fancy for that.

Instead he crossed quickly to the door, locked it, and returned to Trevor Lowe's unconscious form. With some string he bound the limp wrists and ankles and completed the job by forcing a duster into Lowe's mouth.

Then, with a struggle, for the dramatist was no lightweight, he dragged him to the cupboard from which he had emerged, pushed him inside and closed the door. For a full minute he leaned against the door puffing, and then when his breathing was nearly normal, went over to the telephone. He dialled a number and spoke in a hoarse whisper.

'Bruce speaking . . . The game's up . . . Meet me at Croydon in half an hour . . . Yes, 'plane leaves for France . . . Can't stop to explain now. Hurry!'

He replaced the receiver and stood, biting his lips. Then, making up his mind, he took his hat and coat from a locker, put them on, and turning the key in the door opened it and went through to the outer office.

'Greville,' he said with a forced smile, 'Mr. Lowe will be in my office for some considerable time — he's checking Mr. Tempest's account. Don't disturb him unless he rings for you. I shall be back after lunch.'

In haste Mr. Hammerton departed. As he emerged from the doorway of the block of offices he caught sight of Arnold White at the wheel of Lowe's car, watching the traffic and looking straight ahead. The agent turned round and made his exit via the back way of the building.

Three minutes later he was in a taxi speeding towards the nearest public telephone kiosk. While the taxi waited he phoned through to Croydon and reserved two seats on an airliner due to leave on its daily cross-channel flight in thirty minutes.

'Fast as you can, driver!' he barked as he emerged from the box and re-entered the taxi.

Meanwhile Arnold White's patience was growing thin. Lowe had said that he would not be long, but already he had been inside for more than twenty minutes. By the time the twenty minutes had doubled itself to forty he was feeling slightly worried and got down from the car.

It was not his custom to disobey orders, but he felt that circumstances called for it in this case. Anything could have happened to his employer.

With a very determined face he presented himself at Hammerton's offices and was met by Greville, who peered challengingly at the young man over the top of his spectacles.

'What can I do for you, sir?' he asked.

'I want to see Mr. Lowe — at once!' said White, conscious that the eyes of the rest of the staff were on him, or rather his reflection, which appeared in the mirror on the opposite wall.

Greville raised his hands in protest and shook his head.

'I am sorry but that is impossible. Mr. Hammerton left instructions that Mr. Lowe was not to be disturbed . . . '

He gaped open mouthed as the secretary pushed past him and strode to the door of Hammerton's office. That the agent should have issued those instructions seemed proof that something was wrong.

He opened the door and peered in. There was no sign of Lowe or Hammerton. Over his shoulder peered Greville, and from that person's throat came a gasp as he saw the room was empty. White turned a stern face on the clerk.

'Where is Mr. Lowe?' Slowly and harshly he asked the question.

Blinking owlishly and gaping his reactions of bewilderment, he tried to say something, but failed completely. It didn't make sense. He had seen Mr. Lowe enter the room and he had kept a constant watch on the door from the moment Hammerton had gone. How could the man have disappeared?

'Where is Mr. Lowe!' This time White added force to his question. He gripped the clerk's shoulders and shook him.

'I — I don't know!' gasped Greville. I showed him in here and he hasn't come out. I don't know, really I don't!'

White was sure now that the clerk's amazement was genuine. Releasing him he began a search of the office, opening the cupboard as a last resort. When Greville saw the bound figure of the dramatist in the cupboard something very like a gurgle came from his throat.

'Give me a hand!' snapped White, and

between them they dragged the senseless figure of the man out of the cupboard and stretched it on the carpet. It was the secretary who cut the bonds and removed the gag whilst the shaking Greville splashed water over Hammerton's desk in his efforts to fill a glass.

Trevor Lowe's eyes began to open as the young man bathed his face with the cool water. In a minute or two he was sitting up and gently smoothing a bump on the back of his head. His first remark was concerning Hammerton.

'How long has he been gone?' he asked the clerk.

'Gone? Who, sir?' answered Greville,

'Hammerton of course!' thundered the dramatist.

'Over half an hour, sir. Really — I — ' The clerk was completely dazed. In all his years he had never experienced anything like this.

The dramatist jumped to his feet and picked up the telephone.

Arnold White heard him ask for Croydon Aerodrome, but there was disappointment on Lowe's face as he replaced the receiver.

'Hammerton has beaten us to it,' he said. 'He left by 'plane with a lady exactly ten minutes ago. But he won't get far. I'll have the authorities waiting for him when he lands at Le Bourget.'

'Who was the lady with him?' asked the secretary.

'I should imagine Mrs. Tempest,' said Lowe grimly. 'According to what I have learnt our friend Hammerton has been having an affair with his late client's widow for years. That doubtless accounts for the deficiencies in his statement to Mr. Whittlesey.'

He picked up the 'phone again and asked for Scotland Yard, and in a few seconds was explaining to the Commissioner what had happened.

'I'll leave that end of the matter in your hands,' concluded the dramatist. 'My main interest is to find the killer of Roger Tempest. Despite Hammerton's embezzlement of Tempest's money, considerable as the amount is, I don't think he is the man I want.'

22

The Night Prowler

Sombre and imposing against the darkness of the sky Abbey Lodge was justifiably regarded by the people of Minchester as a landmark.

Since the mysterious death of the popular owner, however, an oppressive gloom seemed to cover the fine old house. The blinds were drawn at every window and the servants went about their tasks subdued and uneasy.

Young Malcolm Gladwin was showing the strain in his handsome face. His eyes were heavy and dull; lines had appeared at the corners of his mouth, and his whole attitude suggested a man who has aged twenty years in something less than a week.

Hour after hour Malcolm Gladwin racked his brains for a solution.

He went through the long list of friends

and acquaintances of his father, striving to place a mark of guilt or suspicion against one of them. But here he found himself baffled. Sir Horace Gladwin had been a man without an enemy. At least, that was how it appeared on paper. Certainly no one on the list the young man had drawn up would have gone to the length of killing him in such a dreadful manner. Yet there had been an enemy — obviously.

Only the ticking of the old-fashioned clock in the lounge broke the silence as Malcolm stared gloomily into the fire. When the front door bell pealed through the house he started, and then sighed. His nerves were getting him down.

The butler padded into the room.

'Will you see Mr. Sheldon, sir?' he asked.

'Of course. Show him in, Ward.'

He was glad to receive a visitor, and Sheldon was an old friend of the family.

The architect brought an atmosphere of brightness into the room despite his opening remarks.

'My dear Malcolm, please accept my

sympathy. It was a great shock to hear of your father's death. I felt I just had to come and see you.'

'That's kind of you, Mr. Sheldon. Thank you. I'm afraid I am still rather stunned. I can't realise — You know, of course, my father did not die a natural death?'

'What?' Mr. Sheldon's usually jovial face tensed, and he almost shouted his amazement.

Malcolm Gladwin nodded gloomily.

'He was murdered,' he said quietly. 'I think the police are keeping it quiet for the moment. But we are all satisfied — the doctor, the police and Trevor Lowe — that he was murdered. And the beast who murdered him nearly got away with a 'natural causes' certificate.'

Mr. Sheldon whistled his astonishment.

'Sit down and have a drink,' said Malcolm, glad of the opportunity to talk to someone.

'Tell me all about it if you feel you can,' said the architect. 'It might do you good to talk.'

It certainly did, and by the time the

young man had finished telling his visitor of the amazing discoveries Trevor Lowe had made concerning the doped candle and the letter from the candle manufacturers he had found in the drawer he felt much better. The jovial-faced Sheldon made a good listener and the few remarks he contributed in the telling of the story were of the conventional type.

'You amaze me,' he said for the second time when the narrative came to an end. 'This Trevor Lowe seems to be a very clever person. Pity he couldn't find out anything from the candle manufacturers. You say they denied all knowledge of the letter?'

'Yes,' said Malcolm. 'But Mr. Lowe told me not to worry. He'll get the man who killed my father, take it from me.'

Mr. Sheldon beamed hopefully.

'I sincerely hope you are right. No one would be more glad than I to see the brute in the dock.'

He rose to his feet, held out a plump hand, and took his farewell. When the hum of his car had died away the young man decided to go to bed.

But scarcely had he closed his eyes when the piercing shrill of the telephone bell in the study below woke him with a start.

The voice that came over the wire was gruff, and one that he did not recognise.

'Is that Mr. Gladwin? Mr. Malcolm Gladwin?'

'Yes,' he answered. 'Who is that?'

'I'm sorry to call you so late, but it isn't safe for me to call you or be seen with you in daylight. I know too much.'

'You know too much — do you mean about — about my father's death?' asked Malcolm Gladwin, a curious feeling creeping over him.

'Just that!' was the gruff response. 'If you care to meet me at Tyrell's Barn I'll give you the information I have. Don't, whatever you do, let anyone know of this. Don't tell anyone you are meeting me. It's more than my life is worth!'

The young man assured his unknown caller that he would keep it a secret.

'I'll be there in twenty minutes,' he added. 'Just give me time to dress, and it takes me ten minutes to get there.'

'Right! I'll be waiting in the barn.'

Fired with excitement and anxiety to know what there was to hear concerning his father's death Malcolm Gladwin dressed in record time. Silently he let himself out of the house and walked rapidly to the meeting place.

Tyrell's barn was at the far end of a spacious meadow, and about half a mile or so from Abbey Lodge, and if the stranger wanted secrecy there was no better spot. When he reached the barn he found the door open. The man had said he would be inside.

As he crossed the threshold a shadowy form detached itself from the wall of the barn. A length of rubber tubing rose and fell with deadly accuracy on the back of Malcolm's uncovered head. He pitched on his face inside the building, consciousness leaving him before he reached the ground.

He did not hear the grunt of satisfaction that came from his assailant, and the attacker after making certain that the victim was completely unconscious, pulled down over his face the wide brim of his hat, tightened round his neck the upturned collar of his blue coat, and disappeared into the shadows of the night.

It was two hours later when consciousness returned to the figure on the floor of the barn, accompanied by a blazing headache, He lay still for a few minutes trying to remember what had happened. Then he realised that he had walked into a very neatly placed trap, and with that came the knowledge that his unknown assailant had had the run of Abbey Lodge for two hours!

In this he was right. After leaving the barn the mysterious caller had gone to the Lodge and found to his satisfaction that Malcolm had left the front door slightly ajar. Entering, he had crept stealthily up the stairs to the top floor where, he knew apparently, the domestic staff would be sleeping. Quietly and carefully he turned the key in the lock of each door making certain that there would be no interference from the servants while he set about the task he had in mind. It was because the young man slept on the first floor that it had been necessary to entice him out of the house and so give him a clear field.

With quiet thoroughness the man in the wide-brimmed hat went through the various rooms of the old house, turning out cupboards and drawers.

At the end of an hour he came to a stop, an angry and slightly frightened look on his face.

'I must find it!' he muttered.

But whatever it was he sought, at the end of another half an hour he went away as empty handed as he had come. He left no trail behind him, for his nimble hands had been covered with fine, black, silk gloves, and on his feet were rubber over-shoes with plain soles.

23

Victim Number Three

Mr. Sheldon was enjoying his ease in the comfort of his own private den. It had been a tiring day for him, and the thought of having to journey forth into the rain for the purpose of interviewing the Rev. Horatio Warren was thrust further into the background as the evening wore on.

It was Mrs. Sheldon who ventured into his study to remind him that it was getting late and that he had promised to visit the vicar.

Mr. Sheldon pulled a long face,

'I wish I hadn't promised. I'd give anything not to go out on a night like this.' He sighed deeply and made a half-hearted attempt to get out of his comfortable chair. 'Oh, well, I suppose I must. But it's the last fête I'm going to interest myself in, I can assure you, my dear.'

And then the loyalty and affection of a dutiful wife rose up in Mrs. Sheldon. She smiled sweetly and pressed her husband back into the roomy chair.

'All right, dear. You've had a busy time lately and not too much sleep. You were out late last night — '

'Not out late,' corrected Sheldon. 'I was working here late, in fact, until the small hours.'

'You stay here then,' smiled his wife. 'I'll go over to the Warrens' and do your business for you if you like.'

Sheldon's eyes gleamed with pleasure.

'Would you really — ' he began, and then his plump face fell. 'No, no! I couldn't think of you doing that. It's a filthy night and — '

But Mrs. Sheldon felt very determined, and she liked to be able to be insistent now and again.

'No, you stay here and rest. I shall be back in just over an hour. You wait up here for me.'

This pleased Mr. Sheldon, and his face resumed its jovial expression.

He kissed his wife, lit a cigar, and

settled himself deeper into the armchair.

In a few minutes he heard the slam of the front door. His head was lolling on his chest when, without a noise, the door of his den was suddenly opened. The architect's back was to the door and he did not see the two masked figures.

'That's the man! Get him!' and the next moment the two men bounded across the room.

Sheldon came out of his doze with a start. He blinked in amazement and then started to kick and fight as the men leaped on him.

'Hold him while I get the pad ready!'

Held in the iron grip of the bigger of the two men, Sheldon struggled and writhed unavailingly as he felt a chloroform pad being pushed against his nose and mouth.

'He's going to take it — and like it!' growled one of the men.

Mr. Sheldon took it — he had no other alternative, but not without a struggle. His chair was overturned, the little table with the reading lamp went crashing to the floor and a swinging arm swept everything off the mantelpiece before the potent stuff did its work. Then, helpless, breathing deeply and unnaturally, the heavy figure collapsed in the arms of the two intruders.

'That's that!' muttered the man in charge of this extraordinary business. 'Now bring him out.'

'Why?'

'The Boss gave me instructions. He said to bring him out, so out he goes!'

Carrying their victim between them, the two men crept out of the house to where a van awaited them at the far end of the drive. Without ceremony Mr. Sheldon was dumped into the back. One man followed, and the other got into the driver's seat.

Two minutes later the van left Long Dene, the deluge of rain that now fell affording it extra cover. Few people were out on such a night, and any who did see the speeding van paid no attention to it.

For an hour the van sped eastwards, and then, very deliberately, the driver swung the wheel round and retraced his route. Only when he was within two miles of the house from which he had started did the van leave the main road and enter a muddy, bumpy lane, little better than a cart track.

At the end of this lay Mersham's Quarry, long since abandoned. At the edge of the quarry the driver brought the van to a stop and called to his companion inside.

'Everything all right?'

'Sure!' was the reply. 'He's just come round but I've got him tied up and gagged. Are we there?'

The opening of the van doors by his companion told him that they were 'there'.

'Get him out. We've got to take him below. Ain't he a weight?'

Mr. Sheldon was a weight — fourteen stone four pounds — but between them the two men carried their victim through the pouring rain down a winding path in the side of the old, disused quarry. At the end of the path, derelict and on the point of collapse, was a wooden hut. Into this as if he had been a bundle of straw, Mr. Sheldon was dumped. His eyes stared up at his captors fearfully, full of terror and bewilderment.

The two men glowered back at him.

'So long, Mister. That's our job done. The Boss'll be along to talk to you soon, and he doesn't want us around. Come on, mate' — to his companion — 'this is where we collect twenty quid, and not bad pay for such an easy job!'

The men went out and the creaking door of the hut was slammed to. Mr. Sheldon lay back against the rotting wall of the old hut shivering, and listening to the departing footsteps until they died away. The dilapidated roof admitted the rain, and he lay in misery, wondering how long he would have to wait before help came.

★　★　★

Mrs. Sheldon was glad to be back in her comfortable home. Soon after she had left the house she began to regret having elected to go out instead of her husband. It had rained all the way there, and harder than ever on the way back. On top of it the Rev. Horatio Warren had not appeared pleased to see her, and certainly Isabel had not. Apparently the vicar had not fixed an appointment with her husband for that night. As Mrs Sheldon had arrived, however, the good man did his best to entertain her. She breathed a sigh of relief when she had gone. Glad to be rid of her soaking mackintosh and goloshes she tidied herself before the hall mirror and went into the garden.

'Oh, my dear — ' she began, and then her jaw dropped.

Her startled eyes saw the overturned chair, the table, the smashed reading lamp, the shattered ornaments. But there was no sign of her husband. Then to her nostrils came that sickly cloying smell.

'Chloroform!' Almost in a scream she voiced the word.

With terrified eyes she glanced round the room, half expecting to see her husband lying dead or badly injured.

She searched every room in the house, but could not find the jovial-faced architect she had left sitting so comfortably in the big chair. Sitting in the hall chair, dazed and sobbing, she suddenly remembered that the men from Scotland Yard were staying at the Bull, and without stopping to think of anything else she picked up the telephone and was connected with Shadgold.

'Very well, Mrs. Sheldon. I'll be right over,' he said, and went to find Trevor Lowe.

The dramatist was playing snooker with his secretary, but all idea of finishing the game left him when he heard what the C.I.D. man had to say.

'Sheldon? Sheldon kidnapped!' There was disappointment in his voice. 'That's another theory of mine to be written off!'

'What do you mean? What theory?' asked Shadgold, but Lowe did not answer.

Dragging on his raincoat he and White accompanied Shadgold to the car.

Mrs. Sheldon was standing at the door when they arrived. She was alone in the house, and terrified of what might happen next.

'Now, Mrs. Sheldon,' said Lowe, gently, when they were inside. 'Sit down and tell us what you know. Start from when you last saw your husband.'

Excitedly Mrs. Sheldon told her audience everything that had occurred from the moment she had reminded her husband that he had an appointment with the vicar.

'And you say, Mrs. Sheldon, that the vicar was not expecting your husband — that there was no appointment?' asked the dramatist when she had finished. 'Isn't that rather strange?'

'Well, not exactly. Sometimes my husband's memory does let him down,' explained Mrs. Sheldon.

'Will you take us to the room where you left Mr. Sheldon?' asked Lowe.

All three men were quick to notice the cloying smell of chloroform, which hung heavily about the little room.

'If he was sitting in this chair as you say, Mrs. Sheldon, he must have been taken by surprise, for his back was to the door. Moreover, there were two men here.'

'How do you make out two?' asked Shadgold.

'Well Sheldon is a heavy man,' answered Trevor Lowe. 'And he's pretty powerful. As he's not in the house he must have been taken away, and that would be more than one man's job.'

'H'm!' said Shadgold. 'By the state of the room he put up a good fight.'

'They must have used a car of some description,' went on Lowe. 'Let's get outside and try to find the tyre marks — not that I'm hopeful with all this rain.'

It was Arnold White who found the tyre marks left by the van. The fact that the vehicle had been parked some yards away from the house made them certain that they were the marks of the car used for the purpose of removing Mr. Sheldon. A caller would have parked directly outside the house and not in the shadow of the bushes.

Trevor Lowe examined the tyre impression with his powerful torch, and suddenly straightened up.

'Look here, Shadgold. See that odd marking. That looks like a patch.'

'It is a patch,' said the Inspector. 'We've got to look for a car with a patched tyre

— preferably the nearside back wheel.'

'Why the back wheel?' asked White.

'Because if the front tyre was patched it's fifty to one that the back wheel, following in the same track, would destroy the marks.'

'You're right, Shadgold!' said Trevor Lowe. 'It's a nearside back wheel we've got to look for.'

'Yes,' said Shadgold. 'That's easy — about as easy as looking for a needle in a haystack. I'll get somebody on it.'

Going back to the house of Mrs. Sheldon, Inspector Shadgold asked if he could use the 'phone, and the distracted woman readily gave permission.

Phoning direct to Inspector Mirren, the C.I.D. man gave his orders. The result came quicker than he had dared to hope for. A patrolling car had found a plain van abandoned by the road five miles outside Long Dene. And its nearside back wheel carried a patch in the tyre.

In a quarter of an hour Trevor Lowe, Shadgold and White were gathered round the van. Inspector Mirren was awaiting them.

The inside of the van carried a faint smell of chloroform, but beyond remarking that this was undoubtedly the vehicle the kidnappers had used, Lowe paid the inside of the van no further notice. He examined the wheels of the van and then turned his attention to the driving seat, flashing his torch on the floorboards.

'Found anything?' asked Shadgold.

'I think so,' replied Lowe. 'I think I know where this van has been within the last hour or so.'

'And where's that likely to be?' asked the Inspector.

'Mersham's Quarry,' said the dramatist. 'I was over there the other day. It's a disused chalk pit. If you look on these tyres you'll find traces of chalk, and there is wet chalk on the floorboards of the driving seat. You have a look, Mirren.'

The local Inspector made a careful examination, and then nodded.

'You're right, Mr. Lowe,' he said. 'That's chalk all right. Apart from Mersham's there isn't a chalk pit within fifty miles of Long Dene. There's a grey tint in that chalk that I've only seen in this quarry.'

'Then,' said White. 'I suppose our next move is to the chalk pit?'

'It is!' said Trevor Lowe.

They all clambered into the police car and set off, the local Inspector giving Shadgold the direction.

'Mersham's Lane looks like a cart track. You'll see it if you go slowly.'

Shadgold swung the car off the main road when Mirren pointed out the lane. It was certainly only a cart track, and they were nearly jolted off their seats before they got to the quarry.

Shadgold and Trevor flashed their torches along the ground and were shortly able to find the tyre marks of the van. It was the Inspector's light that found the footprints.

'You stay here, White,' said the dramatist, 'and keep a good look out. This is our way. These prints here come and go, and they are fresh. I'll go first.'

Shadgold and the local inspector followed, and the C.I.D. man had his hand in his pocket resting on the butt of his gun. Lowe kept his eyes on the footprints in front of him, and the two inspectors followed.

The end of the trail brought the party to the dilapidated hut. Boldly Trevor Lowe pushed open the creaking door and swept the interior with his torch.

'Here!' called the dramatist. 'Sheldon is inside and alone!'

Shadgold grunted his satisfaction, and with Mirren entered the hut.

Mr. Sheldon looked a sorry figure. He was shivering and very wet. The relief in his eyes was pathetic when he saw the three men.

Lowe cut him free and helped him to his feet.

'Thank God you found me!' he gasped. 'It's been terrible! Terrible! He was coming back at midnight.'

'Who?' said Lowe.

Sheldon's eyes glittered with fright.

'The Long Dene homicidal maniac,' he said. 'He was coming back at midnight to kill me!' he declared with a shudder.

His words made an impression on his hearers.

'He must be a maniac!' declared Sheldon, his usually jovial face ashen in its terror. 'He said he has a grudge against all the leading inhabitants of Long Dene — all the friends of Roger Tempest!'

'Who is he, do you know?' asked the dramatist.

'I can't be certain,' said Sheldon. 'He did not speak in a normal voice, that I am certain. But I can give you a slight description of him.'

He paused to take a breath.

'Suppose you tell us what happened, right from the beginning,' said Shadgold.

And Sheldon told his audience of the two men that overpowered him in his home, and all that followed.

'When I came to I knew I was in Mersham's Quarry,' he added — a remark that Lowe took notice of. 'Then the two men who had brought me here went off, saying that the Boss would be along shortly. After lying here for some long time the man appeared.'

'Go on,' said Lowe encouragingly, as Sheldon paused.

'He came here and switched a bright torch into my face, nearly blinding me. He stood at the door there and taunted me, gloated over what was going to happen to me at midnight, and then he went away.'

'He stood at the door, didn't he come in to you?' asked Lowe

'No. He stood at the doorway, never came more than a foot inside the hut,' replied Sheldon.

'And can you give us some details of his appearance?'

'Yes,' said the architect eagerly. 'He was a big man, wore a dark blue overcoat with the collar turned up. He had a wide-brimmed hat pulled down over his face. His voice was husky and unnatural, as if he had put it on for the occasion.'

'Dark blue overcoat collar turned up, wide-brimmed hat,' muttered Trevor Lowe, 'That fits the description of the man who did the hospital job, and the man who ransacked young Gladwin's house.'

'That's right!' exclaimed Sheldon.

'H'm!' said the dramatist, and asked no more questions of Mr. Sheldon.

The party left the derelict hut and made their way up to the summit of the quarry. Of the five men Mr. Sheldon seemed to be the most cheerful. Perhaps he had reason to be. He had been drugged, kidnapped, and threatened with death — and now he was free.

In silence the party returned to the architect's house. Mrs. Sheldon was hysterical when she saw her husband, and flung herself upon him, to the embarrassment of her husband and the amusement of Trevor Lowe.

Mr. Sheldon insisted that the others should take some refreshment.

'Please, Mr. Lowe,' he beamed. 'Just a glass of brandy. It will warm you.'

The dramatist accepted, and returned Mr. Sheldon's bright smile.

The smile remained on his face until the jovial man had seen them off the premises, and then his face changed, and hard lines appeared.

'What's wrong with you, Mr. Lowe?' asked the observing Shadgold, when the car stopped at the Bull. 'Why the sudden silence?'

Trevor Lowe yawned.

'Nothing, really. I'm just tired — tired and cross — ' he began.

'Cross, about what?' asked the C.I.D. man.

'With myself — for being such a fool!' exclaimed Lowe, and without another word went to his room.

24

The Vicar's Secret

A distant clock had just struck the half hour, making the time one-thirty a.m. In their rooms at the Bull, Inspector Shadgold and Arnold White were fast asleep, and they would have received a surprise had they known that Trevor Lowe was not in the same condition.

When he had left them so abruptly they had assumed he had retired, instead of which the dramatist was now in the garden of the vicarage.

Stealthily he had approached the long french windows; the curtains were drawn, but Lowe could see that lights were on. The Rev. Horatio Warren was keeping late hours. But that was not all. There were other people in that room, and while he crouched there listening the dramatist made out three different voices.

Faintly to his ears came Warren's voice,

then Isabel's and then one that, although he could not recognise, he knew he had heard before. He tried hard to place that voice, but could not.

Then the vicar's voice again:

'Well, goodnight, both of you. God bless you!'

A shadow flickered across the curtained window as the vicar rose to his feet, walked between the lights, and left the room. A moment later Isabel stood up, casting a grotesque shadow against the curtaining, and in the same moment a man's shadow joined her — embraced her.

Trevor Lowe was amazed, for the silhouetted figure showed a man in a long overcoat, the collar of which was upturned, and in the hand behind the girl's shoulder was a wide-brimmed hat!

The dramatist felt a thrill of excitement. Here at last was the mystery man who must fit into the perplexing puzzle — the key man.

When the man and girl drew apart and moved towards the door Lowe stepped away from the french windows and sought shelter in a clump of bushes nearby.

The door of the lounge that opened into the garden swung wide. He saw the man in the long overcoat and the wide-brimmed hat step out into the shaft of light, which streamed from the room. He moved involuntarily no more than six inches to the right, and then something hard, cruel, and vicious clamped home round his right shinbone.

The excruciating pain and the suddenness with which it happened caught Lowe unawares, and he could not control the cry that left his lips. Even with that terrible agony he did not take his eyes off the doorway of the lounge.

Merging with his cry came the hysterical scream of a woman, and following it came the man's growl of surprise. Immediately the man in the long overcoat crammed his hat on his head and disappeared into the shadows of the garden.

Lowe stooped to discover what had happened to him, and found that he had stepped into a mantrap. He knew that he dare not move his leg to free himself. Bad as the pain was now it would be worse if he attempted to move.

Suddenly the lights in the lounge went out.

'Miss Warren! Come here!' he shouted.

There was no reply.

One minute passed . . . two . . . three. Never had minutes dragged more; never had pain been so terrible.

Gritting his teeth, he tried to move the jaws of the trap. With every movement he made the pain increased. Just as he had decided that it was futile to try any longer the lights in the lounge went up.

The door on to the garden opened slowly. Then in the shaft of light he saw the figure of Isabel Warren. She was in a dressing gown and slippers, as if to suggest that she had been awakened from sleep. In spite of his pain the dramatist smiled.

He called to her again, and then, as if sensing the direction of the cry, she hurried towards the clump of bushes.

'Who is it?' she asked. 'Who are you?'

'I'm here, in the bushes,' said Trevor Lowe patiently. 'Mr. Lowe. Will you find someone to release the spring of this mantrap? Unless something happens quickly I look like losing the use of my right leg.'

'Mr. Lowe!' cried Isabel. 'Are you badly hurt?' Her concern was genuine. 'I'll get father to help you.'

She darted off into the shadows and was gone for about ten minutes. To Lowe it seemed like an hour. His right leg was numb with pain by the time the girl returned with her father.

Nothing was said until the vicar had released him from the trap, and the dramatist winced as his full weight came on to the injured limb.

The vicar was deeply concerned.

'Let me help you to the house, Mr. Lowe. Isabel, you take Mr. Lowe's other arm.'

Between them he was helped into the house. Isabel left them, and returned a few seconds later with a basin of water and some towels.

An inspection of the leg revealed the vicious teeth marks biting hard and deep into the flesh, but no bones were broken. He was silent as the girl bathed and bandaged the wound.

The Rev. Horatio Warren was obviously puzzled. He could not understand how it was that there should be a mantrap in the grounds, and why the dramatist should have been prowling round the vicarage at that hour of the night.

The vicar was embarrassed and did not know where to start the conversation. He looked at his daughter helplessly. The girl coloured and decided to open the conversation.

'I'm — I'm frightfully sorry about that mantrap,' she stammered. 'My father knew nothing about it — absolutely nothing.'

'That's true,' said the vicar. 'I should never have given permission for such a thing to be here. Such cruel things.'

'I agree with you,' said the dramatist with a wry smile.

'I am responsible for that trap,' went on the girl. 'You see I have reason to think that people have been prying round here lately, and that was the only thing I could think of to stop them. I had no idea it could give such an injury. I didn't stop to think.'

'Is there anything around the vicarage that you would rather keep from prying eyes?' asked Trevor Lowe. 'Is it — '

Isabel's face hardened.

'Is it — or rather, is he — a man with a dark overcoat and a wide-brimmed hat?'

He felt sorry the moment he made the remark, for the girl swayed unsteadily on her feet and the colour drained from her face.

'Then you know?' she said in a low voice.

Instinctively her father went to her side and put his arm around her shoulder.

'Don't you think it would be better if we told Mr. Lowe the truth?' he said.

'I think it would,' said Lowe. 'Supposing I help you with a start. Supposing I tell you that I know you are sheltering Richard Tempest?'

There was relief in the sigh that came from both the vicar and the girl.

'Mr. Lowe,' said the clergyman awkwardly, 'Isabel and myself are convinced that Richard is innocent. He did not kill his brother!'

'Mr. Lowe,' said the girl. 'I know

Richard. I know him better than anyone. He wouldn't kill a fly!'

Trevor Lowe smiled at her understandingly. Of course she knew him better than anyone else. The little scene behind the curtained window had told him everything.

'We couldn't see Richard hang,' she went on. 'We know the evidence was conclusive enough, but he is innocent. When he escaped we gave him shelter. We've been looking after him ever since that day.'

'I know, Mr. Lowe, that I have broken the law,' said her father with a quiver in his voice. 'But I am ready to face anyone for what I have done.'

There was a long pause, and father and daughter looked at Trevor Lowe appealingly.

'I suppose it is your duty to inform the police,' said the vicar slowly.

The dramatist shook his head.

'The police do not know, in fact do not even suspect, that Richard Tempest is hiding here. I am not going to tell them — yet.'

Surprise and relief flashed to the faces of the two people in front of him.

'You mean that — that you will keep our secret?' gasped the Rev. Horatio Warren.

Lowe nodded.

'In the circumstances, yes,' he said slowly. 'Like you, I believe Richard Tempest to be innocent. I hope soon to be able to place my hands on the guilty party. I am not quite positive at the moment, that is why I shall not tell the police about Richard Tempest. They would arrest him, and if that were to happen everything I have in mind would be spoiled. Yes, for the time being, I think it would be better if Tempest was to remain 'missing'.'

'Oh, thank you, Mr. Lowe! Thank you!' said the girl, and to the dramatist's embarrassment tears began to run down her face.

The vicar seemed to have lost his voice, but he gripped Lowe's hand until he winced.

The dramatist rose to his feet, ready to depart, when a thought struck him.

'Can you explain, sir,' he said to the vicar, 'why Richard Tempest should be wearing the clothes of a man whose mysterious actions have caused the police a great deal of worry? That long overcoat and the wide-brimmed hat.'

The vicar smiled.

'Both articles belong to me,' he replied. 'The coat is too big for Richard, but it keeps him warm. The hat is an old cleric's hat, which accounts for the wide brim.'

'Thanks,' said Lowe. 'That explains a lot.' He frowned. 'Are you sure that no one outside yourselves knows that Richard is here?'

'No one knows!' declared the vicar positively. 'Would you like to see him?'

'No, thank you,' said Lowe. 'If I don't know where he is I can't tell the police. I would much rather you kept his hiding place to yourselves. I should be going. I wonder, though, if you could lend me a stout walking stick. This leg is still very painful.'

'I'll drive you back to the Bull,' said Isabel Warren. 'Or, better still, let us put you up for the night and we'll get the

252

doctor to come over and have a look at your leg.'

'Thank you, but I think it would be better if I went back. But I'll accept that offer of a lift, if you don't mind coming out at so late an hour.'

25

The Hidden Hand

Trevor Lowe sat in the lounge of the Bull, and his temper was not of the best. Despite the skilful treatment administered by Dr. Bently his leg was terribly painful. He was watching the various people coming and going.

A tall, hawk-faced man had entered the inn. He was signing the visitors' book when the dramatist's attention focused on him. Lowe never forgot a face, and there was something about this one that was strangely familiar, and then he decided it was not the face but the carriage of the man, the way he leaned across the little counter as he signed the book. Somewhere in the past he had met this man.

His temper did not improve. He prided himself on his memory, and now he was at a loss.

Grunting with pain, he put his foot to

the ground and hobbled to the reception-ist's desk.

'Any mail for me?' he asked, without looking at the tall, well-dressed man who was just blotting his signature in the book. It was unnecessary, for directly in front of the man was a mirror which reflected the expression of the newcomer.

Lowe saw him start as he heard his voice, and for a moment there was fear in his eyes. Still looking in the mirror, the dramatist saw the man turn and look at him, watched his face return to its normal expression, and noticed, too, the hard glint in his eyes.

'Nothing for you, Mr. Lowe,' smiled the receptionist, and Lowe hobbled back to his seat, conscious of the stare that followed him.

The receptionist, too, saw the stranger's interest.

'That's Trevor Lowe,' she informed him. 'He's a dramatist, but makes a hobby of crime.'

'Is that so?' drawled the newcomer.

Hastily he picked up his gloves, asked for his luggage to be taken to his room, and entered the tiny lift.

Once in the privacy of his room Edward G. Mansfield whistled his dismay. His first act was to lock the door. Then he went over to the mirror and looked long at the reflection of his face. Apparently he was satisfied with what he saw, for he grinned to himself, and buttoned his coat round him.

'Thank God for plastic surgery,' he muttered.

Edward G. Mansfield, alias Bertram Margerison, swindler, share-pusher wanted by the English and American police, steadied his nerves with a long drink from a flask he carried.

It was his bad luck, he reflected, that he should choose this place in all England and then find the only man he was afraid of right under his nose!

But another drink from the flask, another long look in the mirror seemed to satisfy him. Certainly he did not look in the least like Bertram Margerison. That man had disappeared so completely that the earth might have opened and swallowed him up for all the trace there remained of him.

That had been six months ago, and the police had been forced to drop the case against the notorious share-pusher. A rumour had spread started by the man himself, that Margerison had committed suicide; that he had leapt from a cross-channel 'plane and gone to a watery death.

The swindler had allowed that rumour to sink into the public mind for six months, after which time he had faded from interest. It was safe now for him to come out of his hiding place with a new face and a new name. Doctor Plaistow, famous plastic surgeon, had given him the face and it almost seemed as if he had given him a new life. Certainly no policeman had looked twice at the hawk-faced man, well sun-tanned, who had appeared on the gangplank at Southampton with the customary passport. Everything was in order. A forged passport was not difficult to obtain in the underworld.

While Mansfield unpacked his bags, Lowe, in the lounge, was racking his brains, trying to remember where he had seen the man before. That he did know him he was certain, certain also that the stranger knew him.

He stared rather rudely as the subject of his thoughts came down into the lounge half an hour later. Mansfield returned the stare with equal hostility, though inwardly he was quaking, conscious that the dramatist was running more than a casual eye over him. So he decided on a bold course.

Striding over to Lowe he frowned down at him.

'Might I ask why I am being stared at as if I was a Zoo specimen?' he drawled in a nasal American voice.

Trevor Lowe smiled. He did not recognise the voice, but that was nothing to go by.

'I beg your pardon for being so rude,' he apologised, 'but you reminded me of a man I once knew.'

'Is that so?' said Mansfield with a chuckle: 'I wondered why. My name is Mansfield; Edward G. Mansfield, from New York.'

Trevor Lowe acknowledged the introduction and returned it.

'I'm glad to know you, Mr. Lowe,' said Mansfield boisterously. 'You had a fall off a house or something?'

'Something like that,' said Lowe. 'Will you have a drink?'

'Say, now you're talking my language. I'll have a whiskey.'

The waiter brought two drinks, and Edward G. Mansfield sat down and began to converse easily on general topics. He extracted a great deal of amusement from the fact that he, a very much wanted man, was accepting the hospitality of the person who had been most zealous in his efforts to track him down. But his amusement came to an abrupt stop at the dramatist's next remark.

'You know, Mr. —' He paused.

'Mansfield. Edward G. Mansfield,' said the share-pusher.

'You know, Mr. Mansfield, you remind me so much of a man I once knew. His name was Margerison — Bertram Margerison. Ever hear of him?'

'Never!'

Trevor Lowe glowed inwardly. Strange that this man should deny, and so emphatically, that he had ever heard the name that had been flashed across the world in big headlines. This well-dressed man, prosperous obviously, by the state of his wallet when he had paid for his round of drinks, was certainly trying to hide something.

Lowe signalled to the aged waiter.

'Did you ever hear of a man called Bertram Margerison?' he asked, when the old man came over.

'Hear of him? Like to know who didn't!' he said. 'Dirty swindler. Did people out of thousands and then disappeared!'

Lowe smiled and gave the old man a shilling for his trouble.

Mansfield then realised that he had made a mistake in denying all knowledge of such a public character. He tried to cover up the omission.

'Now I do remember him, Mr. Lowe,' he drawled, flashing his teeth in a wide smile. 'That share-pusher guy, you mean. The man who vanished with a small fortune. Is that the feller you mean? It ain't much of a compliment to me,

Mister, when you say I remind you of him. Do I look like him, then?'

Lowe shook his head.

'No, you don't!' he answered truthfully. 'Your face is quite different. Anyway, he was dark and you are fair.'

But despite the dramatist's easy manner Mansfield was not at all comfortable. It worried him that Lowe connected him with his old self.

He rose from his chair, stating that he would take a walk. Whilst out Edward G. Mansfield made up his mind that if Lowe had rumbled him it was the last thing he would do. In his pocket he carried a small packet of powder, which, if dropped into a glass of whiskey, would stop his activities in this world. On this Mr. Edward G. Mansfield was determined.

Back in the lounge Trevor Lowe was reclining on the settee with his eyes closed. When he came out of his reverie his mind was half made up. He had a strong feeling that this stranger from New York was no other than Bertram Margerison, in spite of the hair and the face. He smiled to himself as he thought of the effect on

261

Shadgold if he told him, and made up his mind to try and trap Mr. Mansfield.

That evening quite a number of people called to see the dramatist. The Reverend Horatio Warren was there with his daughter. Mr. and Mrs. Sheldon, too, were there. The Sheldons were over-whelming in their gratitude for the service Lowe and Shadgold had rendered them. Doctor Bently was there, enjoying half an hour's break from the strenuous demands his practice imposed on him.

The dramatist felt rather like a sick person in hospital on visiting day, but as he saw Mansfield enter the room he had an idea.

' 'Evening, Lowe,' drawled the man from the States, and he bowed to the company.

'Shadgold' — Trevor Lowe was deliber-ately discourteous in not introducing the ladies first — 'allow me to present Mr. Bertram Margerison!'

His eyes bored into the man he suspected as he made the announcement. The share-pusher fell to the bait. His hand made a quick movement to his hip, and the colour ebbed from his face, leaving it deathly pale.

Shadgold was staring at him in utter amazement.

'What are you talking about?' he demanded. 'This man isn't Bertram Margerison. You ought to know that, Mr. Lowe.'

There was a tension in the air, and, sensing it, the dramatist decided to go no further. He laughed lightly.

'I beg your pardon, Mr. Mansfield. You remind me of Margerison so much that I couldn't resist it. Allow me to introduce Mr. Edward G. Mansfield, from New York.'

Mansfield smiled weakly, and the tension was eased in the murmur of introductions that followed.

For the next half hour cordiality reigned, and light-hearted conversation filled the room. Sheldon was in great form, producing a fund of really witty stories.

Only Mansfield was uneasy. He was convinced that Lowe knew who he really was, and his mind went to the little packet of white powder in his pocket. If the worst came to the worst he would use it.

The evening flew by, and Lowe was glad when the company began to break up. On the table next to the dramatist was a glass, half full of whiskey and soda. Trevor Lowe made as if to drink it, decided otherwise, and replaced it on the table. Mr. Sheldon, noticing the action, told Lowe to 'be a man and drink it down,' but it remained where Lowe put it.

A few minutes later the room was empty, and hobbling painfully on his thick stick, Trevor Lowe went to his bedroom.

A dismal-faced servant, cursing the late hour and the amount of dirty glasses he had to clean before his day's work was done, saw the whiskey and, knowing that if he didn't drink it, it would be thrown away, decided to take advantage of this treat.

It was another hour before the Bull was ready to close for the night and it was just then that Lingley began to feel ill. In a few minutes he was shaking as if with fever; his eyes were bright and staring; his tongue felt twice its normal size and his heart beat rapidly, and with it all violent pains in his stomach, which increased with every passing minute. Finally he collapsed on the floor, writhing painfully.

The proprietor of the Bull saw him on the floor of the lounge. One glance he gave the groaning man and then darted to the 'phone and called Dr. Bently.

'Come at once, please, Doctor,' he said. 'He looks to me as if he's dying!'

Lingley was a small man, and it was not very difficult for the proprietor of the Bull to lift him to the settee. The man was moaning feebly now, and great beads of perspiration stood on his forehead.

'I — I think I've been poisoned,' he moaned. 'It must have been that whiskey.'

'Which whiskey?' asked his employer.

'There was — was some in a — a glass when I cleared — '

Dr. Bently arrived just as the man collapsed completely.

He made a swift examination and announced that it was a case of poisoning.

'We must get him to the hospital. Nothing but a stomach pump can do any good, even then it's a question of time.'

Dawn was splashing its crimson streaks across the sky before Doctor Bently rested in his efforts to save Lingley.

'I think the crisis is past, Meadows,' he said to his colleague. 'If his constitution is strong enough he should pull through. There's nothing more we can do now.'

The two medical men left the hospital and went along to the Bull to inform the proprietor of his servant's condition. Shadgold and Trevor Lowe were in the dining room with the proprietor, who had just finished telling them of the incident of the night.

It was Shadgold who pounced upon the facts.

'Didn't you leave a drink on the table, Mr. Lowe?' he asked. 'That must have been the one Lingley had. I didn't notice another when I left.'

'Then,' said Lowe gravely, 'if that drink was poisoned it must have been meant for me.'

'But that's ridiculous!' expostulated the C.I.D. man.

'I don't think so!' replied Lowe. 'Now, Shadgold, who in that company last night hated me so much that they would try to poison me?'

Shadgold was silent for a moment.

'If that fellow Mansfield had been Bertram Margerison,' he said at length, 'I'd say he was the only one. But — '

'There are no 'buts',' said the dramatist. 'You can take if from me, Shadgold, that Edward G. Mansfield and Bertram Margerison are one and the same.'

Shadgold stared at him, his mouth open.

'Are you mad?' he said at last. 'Think I've forgotten what Margerison looked like?'

'Ever heard of plastic surgery?' asked Lowe. 'A clever plastic surgeon can change your face so that your own mother wouldn't know you. Am I right, Doctor Bently?'

'You're quite right, Mr. Lowe,' said the doctor.

'If you're so certain why didn't you give me the tip?' asked the Inspector, and his tone was slightly unfriendly.

'But I did,' said Lowe. 'I deliberately introduced him as Margerison to watch his reaction. I did watch him, saw the hand go immediately to his hip, saw the colour leave his face, and saw the relief when I apologised for the mistake. I'll take my oath that Edward G. Mansfield is Bertram Margerison!'

'Phew!' whistled Shadgold, and began to walk towards the door.

'Where do you think you are going?' asked Lowe.

'To see friend Mansfield, or whatever he calls himself,' retorted the Inspector. 'Obviously he's the man who tried to poison you, and if he is the fellow you think that's reason enough also for me to see that he's put in a safe place!'

'I've got another idea,' said Lowe. 'Anyway, wait for me. I'd like to be in on this.'

He hobbled over to the lift, and Shadgold, with a grim face, pressed the button and they were taken to the second floor. There was a gun in the C.I.D. man's hand as he tiptoed to the door of the room occupied by the man they were desirous of seeing.

As they reached the. door it flew open and Edward G. Mansfield's hawk-like face nearly touched that of Shadgold. He saw the gun, and the colour left his face. He backed into the room, speechless and terrified.

'All ready to go, eh?' smiled Shadgold, noting the two suitcases his man had been carrying and which he dropped to the floor.

'What's — what's the meaning of this?' said the crook, in an attempt to bluff it out.

'No?' said Shadgold. 'Well, let me explain, Mr. Bertram Margerison — '

Shadgold knew then that Lowe had made no mistake. The share-pusher wilted visibly, and his dejection was complete when the dramatist hobbled into the room.

'All right, you win!' said Margerison. 'I thought, somehow, Lowe, that you had tumbled to me. Do you mind if I have a cigarette?'

He put his hand in his waistcoat pocket, and before Lowe or the Inspector could guess his intention he had extracted the little packet from its resting place, torn it open, and gulped down the contents!

Then he smiled curiously.

'I never meant anyone to get me,' he

said. 'I've cheated you now, as I did before! You needn't trouble to get me to hospital,' — as the two men darted to him. 'There's no doctor in England who knows the antidote to this poison, so you can keep your handcuffs in your pocket!'

He coughed, choked, and fell back on the bed.

Shadgold turned to Lowe, who was bending over the still figure.

'If it's poison he's taken so much the better. Only be a waste of the taxpayer's money to bring him up for trial and then keep him inside for twenty years. I'd better get the doctor, anyway.'

There was nothing Dr. Bently could do when he arrived, for Margerison never regained consciousness. The poison was swifter than even they had bargained for.

'It's hopeless,' said the doctor. 'His heart has practically stopped beating.'

A few minutes later it stopped completely.

'Well, Lowe, I think that's how you would have gone had you finished that whiskey. He was the man who put the poison in your drink.'

'You're wrong,' said Lowe quietly. 'White is busy, so if you will drive I'll introduce you to the man who tried to poison me, and then to the killer of Roger Tempest and Sir Horace Gladwin!'

26

Justice is Satisfied

Mrs. Sheldon was more than delighted to see Trevor Lowe and Inspector Shadgold. To the end of her life she felt she would always be grateful to them for saving her husband from a terrible fate.

'Come in,' she said. 'I'm sorry my husband is out at the moment. The vicar 'phoned a few moments ago and asked him to come over.'

Lowe was not surprised. He himself had arranged that Sheldon should be out when they had made their call. A 'phone message to the Rev. Warren had fixed that.

'That's a pity,' said the dramatist. 'But it isn't so important. I really came to borrow his typewriter; mine has developed internal trouble.'

Mrs. Sheldon beamed.

'Certainly, Mr. Lowe. It's in the study.

My husband won't mind in the least, he'll be only too pleased that you came to him.'

Mrs. Sheldon escorted them to her husband's study. Shadgold's face was a study in perplexity. He had no idea what this was all about, but Lowe had promised him to unravel this mystery, and so he supposed it was all right.

Mrs. Sheldon pointed to the typewriter, and told Lowe to make himself at home. When the dramatist sat down in front of it she moved to the door, saying she would get a drink for them.

That was the last thing Lowe wanted, but he did not detain her.

'What's the idea?' asked the inspector.

'I'll show you when I've used this machine,' said Lowe.

He took a letter from his pocket. It was the letter purporting to come from the Gloworm Candle Company. The letter which had accompanied the green candle that had resulted in Sir Horace Gladwin's death.

Shadgold watched Lowe type the letter word for word on a clean sheet of paper.

'Still don't understand,' said Shadgold,

when the two letters were passed to him.

'Use your eyes,' said Trevor Lowe. 'Compare the letters.'

He stopped as he saw the look of understanding on the C.I.D. man's face.

'They are the same! Identical! Good Heavens!' stammered Shadgold. 'Are you suggesting that Sheldon wrote this letter? Because if you are — '

'I'm not suggesting,' broke in Lowe. 'I'm positive. Sheldon wrote this letter! I've had my suspicions, but this type-writer proves it conclusively.'

He rose to his feet and replaced the cover on the machine.

'Come along. You couldn't use your hand-cuffs on Margerison, but you can this time!'

Mrs. Sheldon was very disappointed when she saw that her two visitors were leaving.

'Please wait and see my husband. He'll be so sorry if he misses you.'

'We'd very much like to, Mrs. Sheldon, but I'm afraid that at the moment we are too busy to spare the time. Some other time, perhaps.'

Trevor Lowe felt very sorry for this

woman, and as soon as he decently could he got into the car and they drove off.

'Go straight to the vicarage,' he said to Shadgold. 'We're getting near the end now, thank goodness!'

His tone was so serious that Shadgold did not attempt to ask him all he wanted to know. The dramatist would, at the right time, explain everything, and knowing him, he was content to wait.

The vicar and Sheldon rose to their feet as the two men entered the room in which they were. Interrogation was on the face of Warren. He had no idea why he had been asked to get Sheldon over. But Sheldon was as jovial as ever.

'Hello Mr, Lowe!' he greeted, and advanced with outstretched hand. 'I've just been telling the vicar about the mysterious poisoner who was in our company last night.'

The vicar appeared horrified.

'He might have put it in any of the glasses, mine — '

'Oh no!' said Lowe. 'It was meant only for me. I knew too much about one of the company, and when a man knows too

275

much his enemies try to remove him. Isn't that right, Sheldon?'

The architect shrugged his shoulders.

'I think it was a lucky escape for all of us. When I first heard the news about Lingley's collapse I thought the man responsible was the mystery man who killed Roger Tempest.'

'And Sir Horace Gladwin!' put in Lowe. 'The man who goes about in a dark blue overcoat, Sheldon, and wears a black hat with a wide brim.'

'Are they connected then?' asked Sheldon, and his face had lost its smile.

'They are. You, of all people, should know that!'

Trevor Lowe's hand came out of his jacket pocket and a wicked looking automatic was pointed at the architect.

Sheldon stiffened. His face looked ridiculous in its incredulity.

'You're — you're joking,' he stammered.

'I'm not, Sheldon. I charge you with the murder of Roger Tempest and the murder of Sir Horace Gladwin. Don't move! One step and I shoot! You are going to stand your trial, Sheldon, for two murders, an attempt to poison me, and falsifying the Council's Town planning scheme. Watch him, Shadgold!'

'After our last experience don't you think he'd look better with a pair of bracelets?' asked the Inspector.

'I certainly do,' said Lowe.

The Scotland Yard man had no idea how or where Lowe had found sufficient information to lay this charge, but he knew that the dramatist did not make these accusations without the certain knowledge and indisputable proof necessary. Explanations would come.

The shining handcuffs were snapped on the architect's wrists before he could protest.

'You — you're making a dreadful mistake — ' began Sheldon.

'Of course!' said Shadgold. 'You can explain to the judge about that.'

The man gave a long sigh, as if he knew it was useless to protest any longer.

'I think you'd better ring up Mirren,' said Trevor Lowe to the Inspector. 'He'd never forgive us if we didn't let him know.'

In spite of the handcuffs Lowe had his

gun still pointed at Sheldon. He was taking no risks. The Rev. Horatio Warren stood against the wall gazing helplessly at the three men.

'It seems impossible . . . Mr. Sheldon . . . ' muttered the vicar. 'But what about the mystery man with the long overcoat?'

'That's easy to explain,' said Lowe. 'Sheldon knew you were sheltering Tempest — '

'Richard Tempest? Is he here?' asked the startled Shadgold. 'Mr. Warren, this is — '

'I know,' smiled Lowe, 'But it was necessary to keep it quiet in order to get the real killer. As I was saying, Sheldon knew of this. He had, obviously, seen Tempest in his long overcoat and the particular hat he wore, and made good use of it. That's right, isn't it, Sheldon?'

But the other did not reply.

'That might have been clever if it hadn't been overdone. But in other ways he betrayed himself.'

'But I still don't understand,' said the dazed vicar. 'Mr. Sheldon himself was kidnapped, and taken to the old quarry.

That was the work of the man with the wide-brimmed hat.'

'That was his own arrangement,' said Lowe crisply. 'He arranged that, knowing that he would be found before many hours had elapsed.'

'What on earth did he do that for?' asked Shadgold.

'Trying to throw dust in our eyes,' replied Lowe. 'He nearly got away with it, too. There, too, he made a big mistake. You remember when we found him in the hut, and how very dark it was? Remember, too, that Sheldon said his captor never moved from the doorway and that he shone a powerful torch on his face that nearly blinded him? Work it out for yourself. How can a man in pitch darkness, with a beam of light directly in his eyes, identify a man to the point of describing the colour of a dark coat?'

'Of course,' agreed Shadgold. 'He wouldn't be able to see a thing. The torch would blind him and the man behind the torch would be practically invisible.'

'He made another slip, too, at the same time. He said that his captor was the man who ransacked Gladwin's house. Now no one saw the person who enticed Gladwin to the Barn, and no one saw who ransacked the house, so how could Sheldon say what he looked like?'

'And what about the candle letter?' said Shadgold.

'That was a forgery, as you know. It was typed on Sheldon's machine. Furthermore, on the remains of the candle there were two sets of fingerprints, Sir Horace Gladwin's and our friend here. It wasn't difficult to get a print of Sheldon's and make the comparison. They are identical.'

'I am in the dark about some of the things, Mr. Lowe, how you found all this evidence. I suppose you'll explain later. But do you know why he killed Tempest?'

'Yes,' was the reply. 'Sir Horace Gladwin found out that Sheldon had been falsifying the accounts of the local council, of which he was architect and treasurer. Sheldon decided that Sir Horace's death was better than a curtailment of his liberty, so he removed him, but in a very ingenious way. He put a supposititious case to Roger Tempest, the novelist, and he, unsuspectingly, worked out a cast-iron murder plot — the poison candle. But there was one snag in the foolproof plot. Roger Tempest knew the details of it, naturally, as he had worked it out ostensibly for a story plot.'

'I get it,' said Shadgold. 'The only thing to do to keep the candle plot foolproof was to get rid of the originator of it!'

'Exactly! Which is what Sheldon did. Moreover, he knew of the quarrel Richard Tempest had with his brother, for you remember Roger visited the Sheldons that same evening, and there he saw the wonderful opportunity of removing the novelist and fixing the blame on the brother. I should think that Sheldon followed Roger when he left the house, overheard the final quarrel between the two brothers and made his decision then to fasten the guilt on Richard.'

'Why did he keep him prisoner for over a week before he stabbed poor Roger?' asked the vicar.

'There is only one conclusion to draw from that, sir. Sheldon wanted the disgrace of that dishonoured cheque at Richard's bank to add to the motive for the crime. If that was the case delay was necessary.'

'It's — it's terrible!' said the vicar. 'It's more like one of Roger's thrillers than — than — ' Suddenly a light came into his eyes and he stared at Sheldon. 'Then that was why he kidnapped my daughter. He thought probably that her knowledge of the plot, which Roger had drawn up in synopsis form, might prove his undoing. But, after he'd kidnapped her why — why didn't he — ?' He paused, unwilling to say what was in his mind.

'Why didn't he kill her?' supplied Lowe. 'I think his accomplice, Shorty, must have had ideas of his own. Sheldon is responsible for his death, too. That was no accident. It was deliberate murder. And remember, there, that the man in the dark blue overcoat turned up at the hospital and went through Shorty's clothes to get something that Shorty would not hand over. There's only one thing that that can be — and that is the rough notes of the murder plot. Correct me if I'm wrong,' said Lowe politely to the handcuffed man.

'You're too damn clever, Lowe!' snapped

the architect. 'You know you're right. There isn't much you haven't found out. I gave orders to Shorty to kill the girl and leave her body in the tank. The little rat double-crossed me, tried to blackmail me for the draft of the plot. But I got him!'

'Who set Isabel Warren free?' asked Shadgold, his face a study of puzzlement.

At that moment the girl herself entered the room, and Lowe smiled at her.

'Will you tell the Inspector who freed you from the tank?' he asked.

She looked at her father, fear in her eyes.

'It's all right, my dear,' he assured her. 'You can tell Mr. Lowe and the Inspector all they want to know. Everything is all right now.'

The girl stood for a long minute staring at Sheldon. There was no need for any of them to explain to her. She seemed to know, by the very fact of the handcufts on the architect's wrists, that here was the man who had put terror in their hearts.

'Richard set me free,' she said at length. 'He always takes a walk after dark, and it was by chance that he heard my banging on the inner wall of the tank. I think Richard owes your secretary an apology for clubbing him on the head, but he had no alternative. He was a fugitive with every policeman on the lookout for him.'

'Don't worry about that young man. He's had many worse than that. He seems to thrive on them,' said Lowe with a laugh.

'Mr. Lowe, forgive me for butting in on your party,' said Shadgold in sarcasm, which lost its effect with the smile that accompanied it, 'but would you tell me what Sheldon was looking for on the night he locked Gladwin in the barn and searched the house?'

'Truthfully, Shadgold,' said Lowe, 'I'm not certain. I can only assume that Sir Horace had written out a statement incriminating Sheldon, or that he kept a diary. Whatever it was I don't think Sheldon got it.'

'It was the diary,' snarled the architect. 'I didn't find it.'

At that moment footsteps were heard on the path outside.

'That should be Mirren,' said Shadgold. 'I told him to come here.'

'Well, Mirren will be glad to see Mr. Sheldon under lock and key. The poor fellow's hardly had a good night's rest for a month. I'm tired and my leg aches. There's nothing more I can do. Sheldon is your prisoner, Shadgold. Give Mirren plenty of credit when you get the opportunity, he's worked hard.'

He turned to the vicar.

'Well, goodbye, sir. Long Dene is a far cry from Portland Place, but I hope to have the pleasure of seeing you again. Perhaps' — with a smile at Isabel — 'you will invite me to the next marriage ceremony here. I know that nice people wait until they are invited, but — '

The girl laughed happily.

'I shall expect you,' she said. 'And if you try to get out of it at the last minute, we'll drive to Town and fetch you!'

THE END

THE ANGEL

Gerald Verner

For months, Scotland Yard was interested in the mysterious Angela Kesson, who they dubbed 'the Angel', with her striking beauty. Her male acquaintances had dubious reputations. And in every instance, at the start of each relationship, their homes were burgled and money and valuables stolen. Though unemployed, she lived in an expensive flat, but there was insufficient proof for an arrest. However when her latest escort's home was burgled — he had been murdered, his head crushed like an eggshell . . .

THE TRIALS OF QUINTILIAN

Michael Kurland

In ancient Rome, Marcus Fabius Quintilianus was a real barrister, honoured for being a teacher, rhetorician, jurist and a crime solver . . . In these three stories Quintilian, a character who is based on this early detective, chronicles some of the eminent man's cases. The opening tale, set in the last half of the first century AD, is 'Blind Justice' — where Quintilian must defend a blind man accused of brutal patricide . . .

DEATH SET IN DIAMONDS

Gerald Verner

On a golfing holiday, playwright and criminologist Trevor Lowe and his assistant are on their way to see Sir Reginald Allerdyce. They encounter an old friend, Detective-Inspector Shadgold, investigating a criminal known as the diamond bandit and three robberies committed in four weeks — all involving diamonds. When Lowe discovers that Sir Reginald has been murdered, he suddenly becomes involved in the case. So begins a chain of events that plunges all three of them into deadly danger . . .

THE MAN WHO STOPPED THE DUST

John Russell Fearn

Professor Renhard dies accidentally whilst experimenting with a machine that destroys dust. Meanwhile, when Dr. Anderson operates on a young woman, an accidental slip of the surgeon's knife leads to more than her death. The girl's brother, Gaston — Renhard's manservant — festers with revenge and incriminates Anderson, who is eventually judged as certified insane. When he is then incarcerated in an asylum, Gaston's revenge is complete. However — only Dr. Anderson could avert the catastrophic consequences of Renhard's mad experiments . . .